Cover design by: Matthew N.Y.W.

This book is dedicated to all of those who have been affected by ADHD.

Three important messages to remind yourself and those around you:
One: understand and own who you are
Two: don't believe in everything you see
Three: give any person or situation the benefit of the doubt

CONTENTS

"It is the year 1707 A.G.C. (after the Great Collision)...

Earth has been impacted by the moons of Mars, Phobos, and Deimos, changing the planet geographically. Political alignments have shifted, merging into different "zones".

Global warming has sustained, and the Earth is about to die. Most cities are submerged underwater...

As a last resort to preserve life, the president of Zone One has developed a livable simulation known as the Cyberworld.

Humanity didn't have a choice..."

AN EXCERPT FROM A SCHOLARLY ARTICLE "TO WHAT EXTENT CAN THE CYBERWORLD MOBILISA- TION BE JUSTIFIED?"

CHAPTER ONE

#The Earth is Dying

A set of amber eyes penetrated the dark; and in the darkness, the creature examined its prey with a look of melancholy, but there was no greed or malice in those amber eyes. The creature slowly emerged from its hiding place, but not too much so that the shadow of a nearby tree branch could shade its face. Through his window, Elliott watched the creature with the greatest fascination— and saw, in the merest fraction of light, that those sharp, amber eyes belonged to a cat.

The sky darkened but the cat was still in its hiding place, focused on a mouse that was crawling pathetically, weaving in-and-out of maple leaves. The mouse nibbled on every crumb on the ground, but it never looked up at the predator who was only inches away.

"Go, get it!" Elliott muttered.

And so, the cat jumped out of its hiding space in

one smooth motion and clawed at the mouse and swallowed it whole.

The spectacle ended too quickly for Elliott. He took one last glimpse at the cat, who slipped into a gutter and left the scene, most likely preparing for another attack, and stared at the sheets of paper crumpled before him.

He wanted to resume where he left off and cursed under his breath for being distracted again, for the time was already two hours past midnight. Elliott uncrumpled the balls of paper, having just forgotten what he had written, clenched his teeth as he thought very hard, and then the memory started coming back— he was working on his Social Studies assignment.

The teacher told him that he only needed to choose five questions to complete— out of twenty questions! Elliott couldn't decide which question to do so he decided to do all of them, but this was taking him forever.

It's because of my ADHD, Elliott thought, then he shook his head violently: *No!* He had to stop blaming his symptoms and find a better approach to life.

Then the phone sounded to his annoyance, breaking the peace of the night which he was so fond of. Sometimes he would work until morning, for there was no one to tell him what to do. He had a guardian, but Elliott only needed to check-in with him every Saturday.

He was about to dismiss the notification, but the icon hovering right above it didn't resemble any of the messaging functions he normally used. Elliott decided to check out what it was, just as his right hand tightened— the hand which gripped the assignment and so it was crumpled once again.

The notification popped into the screen before he could even open it, flashing red as the phone buzzed violently in Eliott's trembling left hand. It was a news report from the afternoon which Elliott kept dismissing, but continued repeating every hour. The headline was in red.

"The president of Zone One is about to launch the first step of Cyberworld mobilisation," read the notification. It was weird how the world was divided into zones, Elliott suddenly realised. And then he remembered— and this always fascinated him — it was because of the geographical and political changes after the 1st century A.G.C. (After the Great Collision).

The Cyberworld mobilisation.

Elliott saw the ominous words appearing on his screen. It was a conspiracy theory he didn't want to know about because it was more like another futile attempt to rebuild humanity.

Elliott shuddered but was unable to contain his curiosity: he tapped on the message twice, and the writing transformed into a video. This was much easier to understand.

"Our president triumphs over the completion of the highly-anticipated Cyberworld mobilisation," the video reported, "to those who haven't been following our daily posts and don't know," the voice said verbosely, but Elliott had indeed been oblivious to such affairs, "This refers to a transfer of consciousness from reality to the Cyberworld. Our president claims it to be a mass migration into a world of peace, 'leaving the lifeless planet which humanity has dreaded for so long.' But if the Earth degrades to a point of no return, then this transition of consciousness will be—" the video paused to add emphasis, "permanent."

Permanent!

Elliott couldn't imagine leaving his body rotting in the ash that would gradually consume him whole — but still being alive in this algorithm-driven quasi reality. Was consciousness enough to sustain life—and from a philosophical point of view—were they still human?

The video continued, "The Cyberworld will be launched in an instant. You'll get what you want," said the president, who was walking around the office of the Cyberworld research foundation.

Elliott swallowed and sat a little straighter in his chair. He looked like a typical entrepreneur: average height but very slim; his head was half bald as if he yanked out a good chunk of that greasy grey hair. Behind him, there was a group of journalists, all wearing masks and beneath them— without a doubt—expressions of fatigue and disquietude. But their heads were slightly inclined to the president as if in mid-bow.

"You'll get what you want," the president repeated, his face passive as to not express excitement, but which was already known to Elliott by the high-pitched tone which followed. "Trees and flowers growing everywhere; houses that aren't submerged underwater! A world without hunger and poverty! A world cleansed of its sins and conflict and pandemics!"

This was too much for Elliott. He couldn't imagine such a world, and how it would be like if there weren't issues left to solve. "Suppose everyone was still alive— then they would be spoiled, losing control and discipline," he thought, "they'd become addicted." Addicted— like to drugs or psychoanalysis, or like dependence on technology. No, this was even worse: the Cyberworld is far from technology; it is the prison of life and the human civilisation.

Just then, the president added, "Of course, there must be discipline."

Elliott sighed.

"—the justice system shall not be abolished. Yes," the president finally seemed to smile a little.

"Life and work will go back to normal, but all of this will be observed by artificial intelligence. They're our new companions, the drive of society... each humandroid (a more advanced version of 'robots') will serve one household— and be free of charge!" The president couldn't restrain himself.

"I must congratulate our Cyberworld researchers for developing these beautiful beings— A.I. has never been better!" The president, noticing how the journalists eyed him with astonishment, toned down his excitement.

"By Sunday evening, all of this will be in your hands."

The president was out of control this time. All of this was rubbish! It sounded like a panacea— the theory of finding a general solution to all. Elliott wasn't convinced, but he was also scared.

They didn't seem to have an option, everyone across the six zones had to join this mobilisation sooner or later. There was nothing he could do if he stayed here. It was like suicide! His right hand was balled so tightly he might've squeezed the ink out of his assignment.

Elliott turned towards the window, and the darkness stared back at him. All was silent. The window reflected the clock which struck three. There was nothing except his breathing, mingled with the time ticking in the background.

Then his phone buzzed again, once more breaking the silence he needed so desperately.

Elliott closed his eyes, not sure if he dared to open them to see what other catastrophes the president had created. This project sounded firm and in that instant, did Elliott realise that the president had amassed 500 million followers (almost half of the world's population); he was becoming so influential Elliott was certain of it— sooner or later, he would become a binary configuration, trapped within this game envisioned by this maniac.

And so, Elliott opened his eyes, realising that nothing else could be more frightening than that.

And then, the familiar feeling of apprehension:

this time there was an icon, which didn't flash red but represented his social media account. He rarely used it but decided that it was better to have an account in case someone asked. Hence, he would not appear any more peculiar than he already seemed. Elliott wondered if he knew anybody outside of London who would send him a message at such an untimely hour.

Sure, he was usually still awake at 3 a.m, but he didn't like to get distracted from his studies during the night— everybody knew that. He couldn't recognise this person's avatar, but he accidentally clicked twice and the deep voice of an artificial intelligence said, "Greetings."

Elliott jumped back in his seat, muttering,

"Hashtag: oh, my god."

He wasn't easily startled but there was too much on his mind. In the darkness, he hugged his knees and watched the video from beginning to end— something told him that this was very important, so he tried very hard to focus his full attention. And when the video ended, he thought for a couple more seconds, and let out a shaking breath,

"Oh…"

This was what he heard:

"Greetings,

I am writing to you because there is danger, and you have been chosen to investigate the situation. As we know, the Cyberworld mobilisation will begin in 18-hours. There will be pop-ups around London to distribute licenses and they will be selling devices that accommodate conscience-trans-missions. Do not go there.

There is a deadly virus circulating in the Cyber-world, and this may pass onto people who take part in the mobilisation. A few weeks ago, I participated in one of the preliminary experiments conducted by the research foundation. The virus has been leaked, under the code name: Lucy, but I couldn't contain the spread. It will try to disguise itself when the mobilisation begins.

Not everyone will have seen this message in time, but to all whose attention I have: please meet me at St. Paul's Cathedral at 12 p.m. tomorrow.

We are forming a resistance against this virus. You have been selected based on your high intel-ligence quotient, decision-making skills and emo-tional tolerance. Of course, you may choose not to take part, but we believe that you would be very capable and your assistance could be instrumental to the success of this mission.

Sent by: Anonymous"

So what he had speculated was true! There was an issue with the algorithm and now they needed help. Something told him the message was not sent to many people, and that they didn't want the presi-dent to know. Probably.

Elliott read the message again because the first time had only produced a blur in his head.

Capable? He laughed, what was he apt at doing — decision-making skills and emotional tolerance? That was ridiculous! The email was written to convince him into joining.

And yet, the second person, "you" was too intimate for Elliott. He read over the message a third time, the tone seemed different— it was more sincere. Could it be true that they detected some potential in him? A latent talent? They knew even more about him than he did!

As for the contents of the message, that had produced an even deeper effect: there were only nine hours between now and then— "8 hours and 45 minutes," muttered Elliott, who couldn't help but make some quick calculations in his head, just to be sure, "that's equivalent to 525 minutes!"

Of course, he had to sleep and that would mean another couple of hours lost.

In those few hours, they had to organise a resistance against this virus—

The "virus" was an umbrella term for diseases, biological or technological, that could easily contaminate the body, mind or algorithm. Lucy was most likely a sentient being, one of those humandroids the president was so fond of. This was the most dangerous because A.I. had developed something beyond independent thinking. If these thoughts were spread to the human mind, which was perfectly possible, then that would lead to mental corruption... the melting of consciousness...

Elliott knew these cases were rare, but this wasn't the first time he had received such a warning. He realised the severity of the situation: almost half of the global population could be mobilised in just over 24 hours, and they could all be contaminated.

And another thought struck him— if this anonymous messenger failed to capture the virus, then were they already contaminated? Who would lead the Resistance tomorrow?

Elliott needed to know more.

More importantly, he was entranced by the tone of pleading and desperation in the message. He tried to convince himself that the message wasn't addressed to him and that there would be many others who would sign up to help. But ever since Elliott became old enough to take part in these rescue missions, he always avoided them and regretted that he didn't take part in such events worthy of fame and admiration.

When he was seven, his classmates used to insult him, sometimes unintentionally. Even though he was slow to respond, he understood every word; and every word had an impact on him. Once, Elliott overheard his teacher scolding his classmates, "why did you say those things to him?" she said, "you don't know what he's facing so you need to be kinder..."

—Facing what? Elliott shouted, tears welling up in his eyes. He wasn't easily upset, but he couldn't stand it when people whispered secrets about him behind his back. Nor did he understand why people looked at him strangely whenever he answered a question in class. All he knew was that he felt lonely and... different, and that frustrated him.

He took a couple of deep breaths. His thoughts seemed to clear up in his mind, only leaving a motivation: he was going to learn about the virus and help the Resistance in any way possible.

If he could really join— a fifteen-year-old on a rescue mission! That was a first but he had a lot of good ideas to contribute to the team, and no one could tell him not to do so— he still had a whole week until the next meeting with his guardian. And he was doing something good.

So barely being able to sleep that night with such kindling thoughts, he decided to wake up early and go to St. Paul's Cathedral.

CHAPTER TWO

#The Floating City

L ondon was often described as the last "Floating City"— one of the few places across the
six zones that still existed mostly above
water level, as if unaffected by climate change and
the early meteorite collisions. London was an intricate web of flyovers, barely holding up its Palladian
and Baroque architecture— and all the history in-
vested in it. Only a matter of time until everything
falls apart, Elliott thought. It wasn't always like
that, though.

Focus, he told himself, realising he was getting
sidetracked again.

Right now, he needed all his attention because
he was turning towards New Cannon Street flyover
and this was where he had to stop, but he was
barely able to balance on his hover-scooter, speed-
ing across an array of buildings.

He took a deep breath, and with tremendous

effort parked against the walkway just before a group of people whipped past his ears, nearly knocking him across the flyover.

Elliott was appalled by how badly controlled the air-traffic was, but he also realised that people were especially busy today. After all, the world was being mobilised into the Cyberworld and there was so much to preserve, to study, to experiment with... There weren't usually this many people in the morning, but Elliott saw clusters—up to nine or ten per group, swarming out of every crossroad and dingy alley.

Elliott grasped the edge of the walkway, awkwardly alighting the hover-scooter. His head poked out of the flyover, and he was affronted by the sea —a monstrous blob that consumed everything, the water overflowing with dangerous chemicals, and the putrid smell assaulting his senses.

He rarely came to this area, but that was also because he didn't go out much. He wasn't aware that St. Paul's Cathedral still existed because most monuments were destroyed very early on. So when the message said to meet at the South Transept, Elliott assumed that the person meant some sort of observation deck which oversaw the ancient edifice. Still, he wasn't quite sure if the cathedral served some other purpose besides being a meeting venue.

The map indicated that he had already arrived at the destination, but the cathedral was nowhere to be found.

Was the map outdated? Elliott wondered.

Standing there doing nothing, he saw people on the walkway passing him in a rush, no doubt attending the pre-launching ceremony of the Cyberworld mobilisation. Time was running out! Elliott paced around, starting to panic more and more as people rushed onto the streets. He did not need to see those inquisitive glances to know how silly he appeared—almost like a preacher, but too young and inexperienced to offer any words of wisdom.

"St. Paul's Cathedral dome is right next to you," said his hover-scooter suddenly. A few pedestrians turned around and suppressed a laugh. "Rude," Elliott muttered, cursing under his breath for not lowering the volume of the device embedded in it.

But of course.

The edifice couldn't possibly be on surface level because the water would decompose it. Since the cathedral was so tall, part of it could be preserved in one of those atria— a glass complex which housed an assembly of buildings, also connected to the delicate flyovers.

Elliott looked around him, seeing a small staircase a little further ahead which led to the atrium above— people were walking up there already! Could it be possible that they were all joining the Resistance? Not likely, Elliott thought, calming down a little.

Many people were running up to the atrium with him, others walked out and to another walkway. His map indicated that he was above the sunken

St. Paul's Churchyard, collinear to the New Millenium Bridge Flyover. This was where the cathedral used to be, Elliott thought, squinting at the sea once again.

Not wasting another second, Elliott pushed through the people and entered the atrium, the glass panes above spread-eagled over his eyes.

The sun peeped over the ceiling, but the glass—designed to absorb heat— did a good job of filtering the infrared radiation. Shops spiralled down from the ceiling, and the windows reflected the sunlight into different colours, forming a natural tessellation that led the eye directly to the central focal point.

Guided by these lines, Elliott found himself looking at the rusted dome,

St. Paul's Cathedral.

Finally.

A surge of excitement rushed into his veins. The message was this simple, and it took him so long to find it.

Elliott hurried towards the ancient edifice, which was positioned so that the gold was emblazoned by warm sunlight; and in the light, the intricate design of the cathedral winked at him, tantalising his curiosity and beckoning him to go over.

Elliott marvelled at how the pillars were neatly aligned, interposed with golden statues. He saw that people were peering intently at it, and smiled. They were staring at the pillars indented in the dome's exterior: there were short ones on the first

level, and longer ones underneath, effectively supporting the weight of and barring the entrance to
the cathedral.

A rare sight indeed.

The cathedral was declared as an abandoned site
when the rise of water level had exceeded the capacity; the landmark was gradually degrading underneath the sea. However, they were still able to preserve part of it, as if designed to merge with the
modern atrium complex as a symbolic connection
between the B.G.C. and A.G.C. eras.

"Hey," came a voice that interjected his thoughts,
"watch where you're going."

Elliott realised he had bumped into someone— a
teenager wearing spectacles who was probably one
or two years older than him.

"Sorry," Elliott said, "are you also joining
the.....?"

He nodded, cocking his head in surprise, "Resistance. So you're joining as well? How old are you?"

"Fifteen, and you?"

"Whoa that's young," said the teenager, "I'm
seventeen and I thought I was going to be the young-
est."

"Did you get the message too?"

"Yes," he said curtly, "what's your name?"

"Elliott, and yours?"

"Anthony," he said, looking around him, and Elliott followed his gaze to a short lady standing near
the cathedral. She glanced at them and then back
down at the device in her hands, studying it care-

fully.

Anthony walked up to her, "hello?"

She looked up, "you're Anthony, aren't you?" Then she turned to Elliott, but he didn't expect her to recognise him.

"Hi Elliott," she said.

He jumped back in wonder, how did she know?

Then he stared at the screen in her hands and saw a photo that he didn't know was taken of him, followed by a paragraph of his personal details. He shivered, all of this could be easily tracked anywhere, and there was no longer an emphasis on "privacy", a word he suspected to have been extinct for many centuries.

"Is this the meeting place for the..." Anthony said, but he hesitated at the word *Resistance*.

"Yes, this is the checkpoint," then she brought out a rod and proceeded to scan Anthony's wrist, but he didn't have much of a response.

"What was that?" Elliott asked, alarmed.

"Don't worry," said the lady reassuringly, "we just need to confirm your identity."

Elliott held out his wrist, wanting to get it over with.

"Wait a moment," she said, then moved on to him. She waved the rod and it flashed, but in that instant, Elliott thought he felt something injected into his wrist though he felt no pain. He looked at the spot but there was nothing.

"Alright," she said, clicking something on her device. She gestured to her left— telling them to wait, perhaps? Because there was no one there yet, the people Elliott saw just a moment ago seemed to have disappeared.

But then, an army of shadows shot out from the area in front of them. Elliott looked up in surprise as Anthony concentrated on what lay in front of them — and they saw, faintly at first, a crowd that assembled around the cathedral dome.

Wow.

The silhouettes solidified gently before an iridescent, soap-like bubble, and they approached it slowly. Voices drifted in between the dimensions, and St. Paul's Cathedral stood majestically behind them as if magically calling them into the B.G.C. time period.

But when they turned back, the lady at the entrance had disappeared.

"You haven't seen that before?" Anthony asked, smiling at Elliott's astonishment.

"No," said Elliott, "how is that physically possible?"

"It's a dimensionality lock," Anthony explained, "everything inside will be invisible, people outside can just walk past us without noticing."

"That's intriguing," said Elliott, he wasn't very updated with modern technology.

Elliott recognised some of the people in front of them. They were walking around the cathedral earlier and Elliott mistook their interest for a wonder in ancient architecture.

Apparently not. They were divided into six

groups of three or four, and most of them looked like they were in their twenties. Elliott was glad there were people older than him, but he was also uncomfortable amongst so many adults.

"They're all joining?" Elliott asked,

"Seems like it," Anthony said.

"Why are....?"

"Later, pay attention," said Anthony abruptly, pointing at the cathedral.

The crowd stepped back from the dome, and there was a lady in a brown trenchcoat who walked to the middle. She wore a hood but a set of fierce, amber eyes scanned the crowd. After a moment of silence, she lifted it and her oval face emerged from its hiding place. She examined the crowd silently, and when she turned to Elliott, he thought he saw a look of melancholy... but there was no greed or malice in those amber eyes.

"Come a bit closer," she said, motioning for Elliott and Anthony to join the crowd. She looked around her, and with her eyes off the crowd, she said, "you know why you're here."

Some of the people gathered there nodded enthusiastically.

"My name is Maya," she said, her voice carrying a beautifully dark resonance. The cathedral glowed ominously behind her. "It wasn't me who sent the message but that person left me some instructions about what we should do. But before I explain what we need to do, I just need to make something clear."

The crowd looked attentively at her. All was silent.

"Before you entered this... dimensionality room, shall we call it, Ruby back there injected each of you with a tracker," said Maya, "she probably mentioned that she was just double-checking your DNA because I told her to say that. But actually, we've planted a small marker into your wrist, it's for everyone's safety."

There were a few gasps followed by a succession of murmuring.

"I've heard of those before," whispered Anthony.

"It's a small device that gives us information about where you are and how you are feeling, just in case of emergencies. But this is where it gets serious. If any of you report our activity to the president, intentionally or even accidentally, the tracker can intervene in your nerve synapses and impede your speech. If you reveal too much, then the tracker will stop the electric signals sent by your sinoatrial node. Your heart will stop and you will cease to exist."

The murmuring reached a crescendo but died down when Maya held up her hand. "It may sound harsh but we just want to guarantee the safety and success of the Resistance."

"Wait, does she mean we only cease to exist in Cyberworld?" Elliott asked.

"No," said Anthony, "of course not, it also means we die in real life."

Elliott understood. There could be dire consequences if the president found out what they were doing. He would take measures twice as drastic as this to put an end to them.

When the atmosphere lightened up a bit, Maya went on to explain that the virus was usually diffused via the entrance to the Cyberworld simulation, and this would infect most of the population. Even the fastest solution will take several days: developing a decoder and infusing that into human consciousness.

"What does the decoder do?" Elliott asked. He thought he'd heard of the term before: something that broke down a virus.

But this wasn't the case. Maya turned around and looked at the people standing at the front, "some of us should be familiar with how it works, right?"

They nodded.

One of them said, "it doesn't destroy the virus itself, but reverts the damage caused by it." The crowd turned to him. He appeared to be quite knowledgeable on the topic.

"Do we know what the symptoms are for the virus Lucy?" asked the person next to him.

"We know that the effects can be dangerous if it accumulates for two to three days," Maya said, "dangerous as in, but not limited to, amnesia, poor memory, and a weakened prefrontal cortex which will really impede decision-making and communication."

"Whoa that's very serious," Anthony muttered to himself.

Elliott looked up at him. Everyone seemed to know a fair bit about what was happening. He needed to find out everything as soon as possible.

"What do you think?" Maya asked Elliott suddenly.

"Oh," Elliott said, startled by the question, "yes, that makes sense" He felt the crowd looking at him, his cheeks reddening.

"Well then," said Maya, "can you think of any methods to find the decoder?"

This was his opportunity to contribute something to the team. "Um…" Elliott struggled, staring blankly at Maya, half excited and half frustrated.

"You guys know that the decoder is made of hybrid Si-GaN chips?"

"Well," she continued, "the Cyberworld research foundation has scattered 18 chips around the simulation, across the seven zones…"

Seven?

"Yes," Maya said, responding to the crowd's astonishment, "Australia, which had disappeared long ago, has been recovered in the Cyberworld"

"Anyway, this allowed the researchers to modify the Cyberworld where necessary. If I remember correctly, there are three to four chips in each zone. Some of these are fake, they do not work, just in case the decoder gets into the wrong hands… But I trust that we can find the correct parts of the decoder—and act responsibly with it, right?"

The crowd nodded emphatically again…

Maya rolled out a digital map and showed everyone where some of the chips could be found. "They're usually hidden in landmarks," Maya said, smiling, "I used to work for the president— he has a weird fondness for these places." A few people sniggered.

Anthony turned to Elliott, speaking softly again, "do you have ADHD?" he asked unexpectedly.

Elliott tried to focus on Maya's speech, but the words pierced his auditory range. He choked, taken aback, "How—"

Careful, he told himself.

His guardian said he had improved a lot. So how did Anthony know?

"It takes one to know one," Anthony said quickly, "… no, no, no, I mean my younger brother has it… it-it's nothing to be ashamed about."

"Uh-huh"

"I mean my brother has it and he's the top student in his year"

Oh.

Elliott found his chest heaving deeply, rejuvenation fluttering in his senses— it was true then, his guardian's words:

So much is possible when you truly understand who you are. You're not defined by ADHD, you just need to learn to live with it.

Joining the Cyberworld was precisely what he needed: to understand what he was capable of whilst contributing to the greater good in society.

Presently, Maya said something about "splitting into teams" and the crowd disbanded. She turned to them, and said, "you two, come and join me."

"Whoa, what? We're in her team?"

They hurried over.

"Hey," she said, "how was my speech?" She smiled.

"Great," said Elliott, hoping he didn't miss too much of it. He decided it was better to sound enthusiastic.

"Thanks," she said, "for a minute I forgot what I was saying! What are your names, by the way?"

"Anthony."

"I'm Elliott, what about you?" he asked, accustomed to this polite exchange of names. Even though he knew she was Maya, it was better to ask again.

Maya frowned, "I believe I've introduced myself already."

And then she chuckled, "this is your first time, isn't it?"

Elliott smiled back, politely.

She told them that it was a lot to take in, but they should be proud of themselves for contributing to something so worthwhile.

"We all have to enter different zones in the cyber-world," said Maya, "As mentioned, I've found a secure channel which avoids the virus" She turned to the cathedral dome behind them.

"Is that where it is?" asked Anthony incredulously. He was probably wondering how they could access a half-sunken edifice.

"Yes," said Maya, raising her eyebrows to imitate

Anthony's look of surprise, "there's still a big part of it maintained above water level. Besides, the cathedral isn't linked with the city's cybersecurity system; the president won't know when and where we would enter the Cyberworld. That's why we decided to meet here in the first place."

Elliott smiled at the ingenious idea: the ancient edifice naturally protected them from the president's intelligence groups.

"Using the past to protect the future," Anthony recited. Elliott recognised it as the famous axiom for programming and problem-solving.

Maya turned to Elliott, "do you know how the Cyberworld works?" she asked sceptically.

Of course, Elliott thought, slightly confused by what she meant.

But she went on to explain that it was a replication of the 20-21st century of Earth. "This will make it much harder to navigate, but you do have some understanding of how things behaved back then, right?"

"Absolutely. Ancient history is like my favourite subject," offered Anthony.

The decoder— the landmarks— the seven chips that pieced together to form the decoder. It was as simple as that.

They actually had a chance of overcoming the virus!

"Hurry now," said Maya, "the others are already going to their designated zones. We only have eight hours until the Cyberworld mobilisation begins.

That's when the virus will actively proliferate."

Timer: 7:59 hours remaining

CHAPTER THREE

#The Storm is Coming

Maya retreated a few steps, and in the spot where she was standing the floor was indented with a zigzag. Elliott traced the pattern with his eyes and made out one metre by one-metre square, bearing the shadow of the cathedral dome.

It was a trap door.

She fumbled with a key in her pocket and shoved it into the lock. With a gurgle, the trap door spiralled open and there was a small staircase drilled beneath hidden layers of moss and fungi. They grimaced: the scent of decay had returned.

Elliott couldn't believe it. It was amazing enough for the cathedral to be half-preserved and located in the atrium, but it was astonishing for the shabby tunnel to somehow lead to the monument in its entirety.

The cathedral dome shimmered mysteriously in

the morning light as if there were more secrets to be discovered.

"People are watching us," Elliott suddenly noticed.

"No they're not," said Maya, "remember how we put the dimensionality lock around the perimeter?"

"That's right," said Elliott, embarrassed that he had forgotten.

Elliott peeked into the dark pit, wondering if there was enough space to squeeze through the rusted edges.

He was going to enter, but a chill ran over his body and he was immobilized, mid-step.

It was time.

They were going to leave the Earth in its destructive state, the multitude of life and the footprints of humanity forever erased in reality. It was a sad thought: this could be the last glimpse of the planet he had lived on for all his life. He belonged to Earth even though its beauty and history were complete strangers to him.

He had to honour this planet.

He breathed in, concentrating on the essence of life— the soft buzzing of people around the atrium, the beautiful scent of coffee mingled with smoke, and the rolling clouds far above with the enormous, red sun.

This was something an algorithm could never replace.

"Don't just stand there," said Maya, her voice

carrying an unmistakable urgency. But he disagreed. Sometimes it was better to take things slowly and understand the greater order of life.

They descended a few steps, their noses assaulted by the putrid smell of water and decay. He was savouring the golden minutes the present had to offer, Elliott thought, and he could not waste them.

He took another step, but as he did so, his legs were shaking uncontrollably and he lost his balance...

"Be careful," Anthony warned.

Elliott quickly supported himself against the walls, paused and took a deep breath, then continued, his arms leading him through the darkness.

Forty-four more steps led them into an intersection of tunnels, which were illuminated by a warm yellow glow at the end of each.

"This is much bigger than I'd expected," Anthony said, "so where do the tunnels lead?"

"Different parts of the cathedral, and a subsea network connected to more atria. They're rarely used, only as an emergency exit."

"So the others went to the different tunnels?"

"Yes," said Maya, "hurry now, we're the last ones to get in."

She led them to the first tunnel on their right. They walked quickly towards the distant light source and stopped in front of a red door, "this leads to the construction annexe," said Maya. She pushed through the "do not enter" sign, and they stepped onto an uneven ground of metal beams.

"Whoa," said Anthony. Stepping into the cathedral was like stepping into an alien world.

A giant beehive-shaped dome with a tall, shaky ladder leading up to it, loomed into their view. It was covered with yellow and grey strokes, but the rest was washed away with time.

The warm colours of the dome complemented the faint light that seeped from the atrium through the windows. The dome was circumscribed by ringed structures and elegant arcs that formed a complete rotational symmetry. But the pattern didn't end there.

They peered intently through the scaffolding and saw the sturdy pillars forming more arcs and hexagonal formations that cornered three or four entrances to the cathedral. A wave of debris clouded the floor, isolating a star-like structure that gaped at them, enigmatic and menacing.

"So it was never flooded then?" asked Elliott in awe.

"Apparently not," said Anthony, "what a shame we can't see what's beneath all that mess. It would've been quite significant because St. Paul's cathedral has also housed many cultural and religious ceremonies..."

Elliott brought his attention back to what lay in front of him: sitting squarely beneath the dome were what seemed like surgical chairs. They jutted out from a heap of collapsed church organs, and special helmets were dangling askew over them.

Maya hurried over to a panel near the chairs and

tapped in a sequence of letters and numbers, resembling coordinates. The machine roared as she turned on the power source.

"Come," she said, adjusting the chairs so they inclined in a comfortable position, "everything's been set up". Elliott and Anthony followed her and sat down on the closest ones. Directly above them now, Elliott noticed how serene the cathedral dome looked, filled with the memories of human life if not the evidence.

Anthony and Maya grabbed onto their helmet and Elliott did the same.

"Are you ready?" Maya asked.

Elliott sighed and pulled the helmet over his head, shutting all sight from his eyes. The soft texture against his face told him it was an anaesthetising cap. They were quite popular in surgical operations, even minor ones as it minimised the perception of pain and reality. Elliott shuddered: what impact did this have on the human mind when used in the long-term?

A buzzing sound started, and droned in his ear, shaking the helmet altogether as if it was about to explode. He felt numb, his body trembling but senseless to control it. He waited in the dark behind his eyelids, anticipating— all of that anticipation from the moment he answered the message was building steadily...

Presently, a blur of white started entering his vision, then there was a spark, and everything spiralled into fireworks.

There was no going back now.

Lines formed and trees took shape, green like never before quickly painted on the white canvas in his mind. Blue spots appeared and Elliott saw a river, crystal clear like drinkable water, forming and converging with more greenery. The sky descended upon the horizon with a faint yellow— calm sunlight which radiated with comfortable heat.

And then his senses returned to him, a feeling of insouciance that was being introduced to his human soul. The world was unfolding like the wings of an eagle, beating like the heart of a newborn, a power equivalent to the universe rolling to its end.

Ah-h-h...

Never had the atmosphere been so light and the ground below his feet so soft. There was a gust of cool wind and the purest scent of chlorophyll.

The president was right, trees and flowers were growing everywhere— and there were houses! Small dots of red and brown covered the distant hills and seas.

"Maya, Anthony, are you guys there?" Elliott cried out happily. He had never seen anything so purely natural.

"Yes I am," said Anthony, "this is beautiful!"

Someone tapped his back and Elliott spun around, laughing. It was Maya, smiling, her amber eyes glittering in the yellow sun.

"I've never seen water so blue," said Elliott. The sky and sea merged into one, an archipelago of trees and rocks jutted out from both sides.

"They say this was how the world used to be," said Maya, her voice and amber eyes peeking out of the trees.

Elliott ran towards them, breathing in the gentle breeze and sunlight; and he ran effortlessly, guided by nature like gas expanding into the sky.

"Amsterdam," said Anthony suddenly. They turned to him. "Amsterdam, capital of the Netherlands, the city of light interspersed with canals, guided by the scent of tulips and the sound of bicycles!" He smiled, "that was what I read from an ancient history magazine."

"That's correct," said Maya, "Amsterdam was one of those places submerged underwater A.G.C." She looked at the canal, smiling wistfully, "it's a shame, isn't it?"

Amsterdam.

The name reverberated in his mind as he marvelled at the splendour before him, the still image of nature at its finest, swaying with the calmness of the world. Humanity needed nature; the two have been alienated for too long.

"Wait...I thought we were going to Paris?", asked Elliott, coming out of his reverie.

"No. If my hunches are correct, the Zone One chip will not be hidden in the major satellite (Paris), so I thought we'd try Amsterdam first," reasoned Maya.

"Do we just walk like this?" asked Elliott, prodding the ground beneath his shoes.

She nodded, taking the lead and marching into the grass.

"Elliott, what are you doing?" a voice suddenly cried, it belonged to Anthony. Maya turned back impatiently, they were already ten to fifteen metres ahead of him, their figures shaded by the sun.

How did they get there so quickly? Elliott wondered as he walked a bit faster. He was distracted again, so he told himself that the circumstance was urgent.

Urgent.

They were building the bridge between past and future, a bridge chained to billions of lives, each carrying a fragment of the human civilisation, its biological and spiritual essence congregating...

That was an enormous responsibility.

Focus, Elliott.

The Cyberworld was corrupted, and Elliott understood why. He doubted if there would be control facing a world with life so incongruous to their own. And now he saw the effects: he was addicted, disorientated, ignorant of the present dangers they were facing. He knew those seconds of distraction would cost him dearly.

He ran quickly and joined them, but just as he did so, a powerful force gripped his body and he turned around, unexpectedly staring at a tower they never knew was there. There was a tingling in the wrist that made him look in that direction— all of them.

The convulsion only lasted for a second, and when it left Elliott felt an inexplicable sense of déjà vu.

The building carried the resemblance of a bacteriophage— a sturdy cuboid structure with a twisted roof, and a small top that stuck high into the air.

"The A'dam tower," said Anthony, a name that was weirdly familiar to Elliott, "it used to be the office of a Dutch oil company, became a tourist destination, then was further elevated to a global landmark in a succession of centuries."

Elliott knew he had never seen the tower— Amsterdam didn't even exist in their epoch, except in the #FeatureFriday ancient history magazines. But there was a faint connection that called his mind for answers, a ringing in his wrist. He felt drawn to it.

What was happening?

"You're feeling it," said Maya, as if reading his thoughts, "the subliminal sense, driven by the tracking device we implanted in you."

Anthony frowned in thought, "what can it do?" He asked, just as concerned as Elliott.

"The tracking device launches on one of the neuron synapses. It may monitor and to a lesser degree influence your thoughts, and let's not forget everything else I mentioned in my speech," said Maya, "but it can also develop connections with nearby radio waves and microwaves..."

"Thereby helping us communicate with other groups," said Anthony, finishing the sentence.

"Exactly," said Maya, "more importantly, it can help us detect the hybrid Si-GaN chip which we need to find. You'll see that a rough version of the map is etched onto your skin. Right now, it is telling us that it is somewhere in the A'dam tower..."

Elliott looked sceptically at his wrist and found a set of dots, one blue and one red, inked onto his skin.

"The red dot is the location of the chip, and the blue dot is our location?" Anthony guessed.

"Yes," said Maya, "but don't worry, it's perfectly safe."

Perfectly safe, a tracking device?

He remembered Maya explaining that it showed where they were and how they were feeling in case of emergencies. Not only that, it was a defence mechanism against the president in case anyone leaked important information— something Elliott no longer thought was reasonable.

For the safety and success of the Resistance! No, they were taking this too far by adding the subliminal sense, it devalued their natural capabilities in problem-solving and instinctive nature, and they couldn't depend on it. He understood that this was the Resistance, and they carried an enormous responsibility; drastic measures for drastic conditions, he thought. Still, nobody knew about these other functions until now, and that frightened him.

"Go," said Maya, "now that we've detected the location we must hurry." She started running again, and Anthony followed, just as quickly. Elliott tried to focus on them so that he wouldn't be behind again. But in a few seconds, Maya was already lost in the shadows of the trees, and Anthony was a good five metres ahead of him.

Elliott's heart pounded quicker, he didn't want to drag them down. He continued running, but the thought of the tracking device and the subliminal sense burdened his mind. He couldn't help but look at the mysterious tower on his right and study it to know how much further they had to run.

"Are we almost there? What do we do when we get there?" Questions left Elliott's mouth before he could even focus, and he trembled... trembling with the houses as they rose from the green slope.

"Maya," Anthony called, "slow down a little, will ya?"

Maya stopped, her face darkening with the light. Her figure grew larger again. She looked up at the sky every now and then.

"What is it?" Elliott called, unable to conceal his distress.

"I don't know," she said, "something's off..."

Elliott followed her gaze to the three windmills diametrically opposite to them. They were flashing sporadically, casting feeble rays of light into the sun-shattered river. Where Elliott hadn't noticed until now, rose the three towers, with blaring gleams spinning around randomly, cutting through the peace of the wild.

And then behind these cries of alarm shadows overtook the blue and green; and like a pack of wolves, the grey clouds descended ominously. The windmills evaporated and gave way to a howling wind which tremored the earth and sea.

Silent still, they continued walking, but the grass muffled their footsteps. Elliott was running out of breath, he could feel his chest heaving in and out forcefully, an accumulating tension as he waited...

Bang!

Eliott turned around with an instant seizure in his heart, his ears were tuned to that lethal sound— an explosion. What was it?

He looked at Anthony for answers but he only shrugged. Then he examined a pack of willow trees, his suspicions forming silhouettes before his sight, but there was only emptiness before him...

Bang!

The sky turned black with a deafening crack, there was a shriek, there was a web of lightning that reglowed the river, like flames rekindling before the ashes...

Elliott quivered, caught by surprise again. He looked around to see what had caused the disturbance, helpless amidst uncertainty.

"What happened?" Elliott asked.

Maya shook her head in disbelief, "Albert's team — group seven— has been ejected from their zone, Australia, and the president's Cyberworld Security Intelligence C.S.I. had detected some disturbance when we entered. They've hijacked the weather system," she said quickly.

Are they being watched?

Elliott shuddered, wondering if the C.S.I. knew they were here. Everything could be easily observed in the Cyberworld, but only if they knew where to look. What consequences did they have to face if they were discovered?

Consequences, how ironic.

They were protecting the Cyberworld from the virus. Yet the president thinks people are trying to sabotage the mobilisation into the cyberworld. He doesn't even know how flawed his algorithm is!

Anthony's brows furrowed as well, as if sharing the same thoughts.

"But we still need to go to A'dam tower, don't we?" Elliott asked.

"We must," said Maya, "and before the C.S.I. sends agents to guard the decoder chip."

"But what happened?" Elliott tried to ask again. Why was the group ejected? Were they safe? Who was going to step into complete their task?

"Someone has betrayed us," Anthony speculated.

"No time to dwell on it," said Maya, "we need to get there right now. We need to— we need to find shelter."

Her voice was broken up by the wind.

The air became musky, and they had to rely on their senses to navigate through the haze. A wave of blackbirds skidded over the trees and soared bravely towards the decaying sun. The sea rippled and the ground rumbled, rodents weaved in and about the tall grass.

Elliott turned to Maya but she had already leapt into the shadows like a leopard. Anthony followed, looking back now and then and waved his arms, signalling for Elliott to move faster. But the wind roared and he couldn't catch a single word he said.

How did everything change so rapidly? Every step Elliott took was like entering another world.

This was only a glimpse into the faults of the Cyber-world, its feigned beauty, whether designed intentionally or not, baiting the mice into the trap. He was stronger than this, he told himself.

Out of the corner of his eye, Elliott saw a mass of tree branches flying towards him like raining arrows. His legs buckled, he was too slow to respond, still looking at Anthony who begged him to run... he was gasping for breath, and he stumbled as the arrows pinned him to the ground.

Maya was running back.

Elliott urged through the sea, but stronger waves eroded his path; he went back two steps for every step he took; he was trapped in the wind and the rain and the flying debris.

Come on!

He didn't want to disappoint Maya and burden the team, and yet there was nothing he could do to escape the wrath of the storm.

Maya braved the sea and was running back,

"Elliott!" she called.

Elliott couldn't see; the wind blurred his vision and the world was flying around him. He mustered all the energy he had in him to stay calm... most accidents occur when people lose their sight and act irrationally. Sight was the vulnerability of humans and Elliott had to control this. He relaxed his muscles, trying to use his subliminal sense to guide him. There was a flicker in his wrist, but the fire was extinguished by the commotion inside and around him...

Then a hand grabbed onto him; a strong force tugged him out of the drowning sea. Elliott opened his eyes, pushed through the soil and the grass, and ran towards his lifeguard. Maya kicked through the mass like a swan and brought Elliott away from the river, where all light was being swallowed.

"Thanks", said Elliott, trying to catch his breath, urging Maya to slow down.

Maya didn't reply but motioned for him to run— to run out of the storm, to run towards the houses where there were safety and shelter.

It was lucky that he stayed calm. But the fact that they were dependent on fate reminded him that he was balancing the beam of everlasting life and death; he had to push through so that he could eventually land on the safe side.

With this thought in mind, Elliott ran, but his lungs were burning; Elliott ran, but his legs were sore and shaking from the cold and they couldn't carry on much longer; Elliott ran, wanting to prove to Maya and himself.

Maya still held onto him, forcing him to run and not look back.

A colony of houses rose from the sinking horizon, their red and brown roofs shaking as they ran, the world always spinning in front of them.

They continued slowly and Maya released her grip from Elliott's arm.

"Where's Anthony?" she exclaimed, in an unusually high-pitched voice connoting to annoyance.

"Calm down a little," Elliott pleaded, "wouldn't he be at the A'dam tower already?"

"No," she said with the same tone, slashing the air with her hands, "the subliminal sense doesn't work like that. The waves are distorted in these weather conditions."

"You, stay here," she said, trying to master her cool. She ran around the houses in front of them, inspecting every road squeezed in between them. Then she went back to where they started, cruising effortlessly through thunder and lightning.

Finally, she came back, "you might be right," she huffed.

Feeling exasperated, Elliott almost blurted out, *told you so!* But was reminded by his guardian's words that this was only an exclamation of arrogance and self-assertion.

It was hard to see where they were going, so Elliott tried to focus on his subliminal sense. He took in a deep breath, and as he exhaled, the vibration in his wrist started growing stronger, pointing him in the correct direction as it did before. Right now, the tower was calling him with unmistakable urgency. They had to retrieve the chip before the president sent for the C.S.I.

Maya followed him, and he could see her expression of surprise, if not... pride in his peripheral vision. Think of Anthony's younger brother, he told himself. Indeed, *they* were not to be underestimated. He had to prove to the world what ADHD truly meant.

With that renewed morale, he took the lead and slowly, they found their way back to the canal and followed the path they were originally taking. When they arrived at the first crossroad, marked by fallen trees, Elliott didn't stop but knew to turn towards the bridge which crossed over the canal. Reluctant but out of curiosity, he checked his wrist and saw that the blue dot was now much closer to the red.

As he stepped onto the bridge, he was once again affronted by nature, the wind slapping his face as the water currents cursed at him from both sides. This time, the wind carried his steps and he broke into a jog. He was still attracted to A'dam tower in an unfathomable way, but he gained control over the tingling sensation, propelling it to increase his pace.

Maya followed just behind, their steps soft and steady against the stone-tiled bridge, and their shadows drawn into parallel lines.

Now he made a turn to the left, and an arena of buildings populated the horizon, the houses colonising the trees. The A'dam tower was directly in front of them now, obstructing the sky and leaning over with a regal bearing.

It was a few hundred meters away and in the subdued light, the glass tiles were shining like the coils of a snake—a predator that loomed over their view.

Now, they were only within a few strides of the tower, surrounding it were acres of grass that rose like soldiers.

The pulsing in his veins stopped there, and so did his subliminal sense. They had arrived at the enigmatic monument. Elliott looked above him, his eyes climbing the scales of the building. At the very top, as if twisted from the tower's main structure, there was a cuboid that projected from all corners. Hovering above the clouds, it was there that the force radiated over thousands of kilometres and drew them in.

Elliott was dripping wet— both of them were. They stood together, their liquid shadows consuming their muddy footsteps.

"Do you see Anthony?" Elliott asked, peering intently through the entrance. All was dark inside as if the tower was under construction.

"Anthony, where are you?" Elliott shouted.

"Quiet," said Maya sharply, "we don't know if there are other people."

Elliott's mind started racing again, he had to think about the C.S.I, but also about Anthony— where else would he be, if not the A'dam tower.

"Elliott! Maya!" Came a voice around the corner.

They let out a sigh of relief.

The tall figure emerged from the road Elliott and Maya just came from, "how did you know I was here?" asked Anthony, his face ghostly white under the grey clouds, as if he barely escaped the storm himself.

Elliott smiled, but he didn't want to boast in front of Maya, although she didn't say anything, "just guessed," he said finally.

Maya approached the front door slowly, her solitary shadow emerging from the pack. She paused before a sign in front of it and whispered something to herself, nodding in deep thought.

Elliott thought he knew what she was thinking:

This was it.

This was where part of the decoder was; part of the solution to the virus which haunted the remnants of humanity. All of his struggle and anticipation had finally brought them to their destination, forming a single ray of hope and determination.

"Welcome to A'dam tower," said an android out of the blue. They jumped back in surprise. They had gotten too close to the entrance and the door slid automatically before them.

Elliott and Anthony laughed nervously.

And then, the interior was lit with a warm, yellow glow, revealing the hexagonal structure of the ground floor. The chairs were still stacked up in one corner, there was a rectangular bar table and a collection of bottles behind it.

Maya entered the lift softly and held it open without looking at them. Something was still wrong.

"Welcome to A'dam tower," said the same drone again, "which floor—"

Maya pressed the highest floor, "now finding the chip is only the first step—" She started, but there was a reverberating sound that interjected.

Suddenly, the walls of the lift turned yellow and there were bursts of multi-hued neon lights. The colours tessellated along the vertical tunnel, forming a diamond, then a circle, and finally a massive emoji popped right above their heads.

"Is that an emoji?" Elliott laughed.

"Yes," said Anthony, "back then, emojis used to be quite popular, the craze of the new age and often associated with social media. The smiley face is quite creepy, huh?"

Maya smiled a little, but she was unimpressed.

Timer: 6:00 hours remaining

CHAPTER FOUR

#Over the Edge

Something was off.

They stood silently in the elevator, waiting for the music to finish. The cable rolled to a stop with the drone saying, "welcome to the 360° sky deck, with the Panorama Restaurant & Rooftop Bar and the Swing... Over the Edge".

The doors rolled open with the wind soaring past their ears. The rain had stopped and the skyline of Amsterdam rippled in the sea around them.

Elliott ran towards the edge of the roof, impatient. Anthony would have been thrilled, but his face was still pale with a million thoughts.

Miles of buildings stretched out in all directions, low-lying so that the detail of every one could be easily perceived. Boats floated like a thousand seagulls and white hats, highlighting the matrix of canals that flowed through the city. On the other side, the trees formed territories here and there, and green plains intertwined with the water like veins and arteries.

But the darkness overruled this beauty, and so did the throbbing in his veins. Elliott's subliminal sense was returning, stronger than before. This was where they were supposed to be, but an eerie aura dominated the skies above them.

"The chip," said Maya, "do you guys feel it yet?"

"Let's spread out," said Elliott, "in half a minute, we could walk around the entire perimeter". Maya nodded. Patience, Elliott thought, that was the key to finding where the chip was.

Elliott walked around the corner and saw a set of construction beams which looked like cranes. But the red chairs dangling over them told him otherwise. He shuddered at the idea of sitting there and being swung over the roof, but again, he wasn't very familiar with how life used to be. Perhaps, being swung off a high building with the possibility of imminent death was considered fun?

He walked towards the swing as Anthony came from the other end. But as they approached, the chair started lifting into the air, fraction by fraction, shaking just the slightest bit as they did so. He felt a reverberation in his wrist and he realised that it was all connected. The tension was so strong now, he could almost perceive the waves radiating from the chair, and the chip tucked underneath it calling to him.

Anthony nodded at him, "it's there."

Elliott bent carefully towards the swing because

the connection to his wrist was so strong the slightest movement could send the chair flying over the tower. He let out a shaking breath...

So delicate!

He examined the back of the chair, seeing a compartment and sensing a melodic tinkling inside that belonged to the chip.

But it was locked.

Four screws pined the compartment neatly beneath the chair, and it was impossible to yank it out without causing the whole structure to collapse. Perspiration gathered on his forehead as he squatted behind the swing.

But as he moved to the other side to continue working, there was a glimmer in the corner of his eye that caught his attention, his face turned towards what lay beyond the fence, and he was affronted by something very inconceivable

"Hashtag: oh, my god."

He got up but with a sharp smack, he hit his head against the chair. Ignoring the pain, he approached the edge, wondering if what he just saw was a hallucination.

Look down, he dared himself. Indeed, his eyes had not deceived him the first time. One of the weirdest sensations filled his body as he stared into an oval portal-like fabric that clouded everything from below. It was a cluster of nothingness! An eruption of solitude! A multitude of events that overwhelmed Elliott's mind.

"Is everything alright?" asked Anthony, peering

nervously at him.

"I don't know," said Elliott, still concentrated on the floating substance just over the deck.

He pointed to the chair, "there's a small compartment, I think it might be locked."

"Maya," Anthony called loudly.

"Quiet," Elliott hushed, reminding him they could potentially be under surveillance by the C.S.I.

But he had to focus on the scene, he wanted to think about it himself because something strange had overcome him— he found himself incapable of telling Anthony about it! It was as if he had a special connection with the gaping portal.

Yes, a portal. That was what it seemed like.

And through it— and through it! He saw another world— blue seas, green trees. But in the middle, there was a giant building with obvious influences from the 20-21st century modernist and expressionist architectural movement. The structure was laced with white shells, resembling one of those military bases the president created on the Kepler planets.

Frightened— no, that was far from what he was feeling. What went on in his mind was a myriad of emotions. In that instant, he realised so much was possible in the Cyberworld. There were no limits because humanity favoured indulgence over discipline. They could probably teleport to any place, even a fictionalised world like this one!

Maya hurried over, "is everything okay?" she asked. Anthony showed her the compartment they had found. Elliott walked away from the fence, deciding to stay on track with the task. He didn't want to think about it anyway.

Presently, Maya took a small blade out of her pocket, except the handle was round and there was a small shaft protruding out of it.

"It's a screwdriver," Anthony said, seeing his look of interest.

Maya positioned it carefully beneath the seat, breathing in and out rapidly, she could feel the disturbance as well. The shaft and lock connected perfectly and she twisted her wrist a little. Her hands moved quickly around the compartment, and then there was a small click and a thud on the floor.

Embedded in the corner of the box was a small chip, roughly 2 x 2cm in size. Maya pinched it out and lay her hand out flat for everyone to see. They huddled around, holding their breaths, realising that this could be one of those fake chips. All of that hard work for nothing!

Elliott and Anthony stared at Maya anxiously, and she inspected the pattern inscribed on the surface.

"If my instincts are correct," she said, "the bar code has seven digits as opposed to six in a nonfunctional one." "Yes," she said, more certain now, "it's real."

They looked at each other excitedly: if only the other groups did the same then they would be nearly finished!

"Stop what you are doing," said a deep voice

that resonated across the roof. Elliott felt his throat constricting— the indescribable fight-or-flight response whenever he was caught doing something suspicious.

They turned around slowly, Anthony lifted his arms above his head. Two agents wearing neon red jackets stood firmly in front of them, barring the entrance to the lift.

The taller one held up his hand, palm facing them projecting the words, "the Cyberworld Security Intelligence," and said, "what were you doing over there," he pointed at the "over the edge" chair swing.

They stood there speechless, still recovering from the surprise appearance of the C.S.I. Elliott swiftly calculated the distance between them and the guards: around five metres, still within shooting range. But there was nowhere to run, they were already backed up against the swing behind them.

Silent seconds ticked by, making them look more and more guilty as time passed.

The guard levelled an inquisitive gaze.

Quick! Elliott racked his brain for an answer, a lie perhaps. He didn't know what the C.S.I. was capable of doing, in terms of threats, but only knew to use his spontaneity to his advantage.

Elliott wondered if the agents actually knew what the decoder was, or where the chip was placed. Because behind the stern expression the taller one's eye twitched a little, betraying an air of uncertainty.

No, he didn't know what all of that was, it was sensitive information the president would never release. He could feel his ears ringing, he had found their blind spot, now he just had to pitch it well...

"We were just inspecting the tourist destinations," he started, feeling Maya, Anthony and the two agents looking at him. He had to maintain his cool and modulate his voice with more confidence. "Don't jump so quickly to conclusions," he said, adding a bit of arrogance to his tone, "the mobilisation will happen shortly so we just had to make sure everything was okay."

"That's right," said Anthony, continuing the tone he used, "we're workers from the Cyberworld Research Foundation."

Elliott could see the stocky guard recoiling a little. If they arrested the wrong person, someone who had close ties with the president, then they would be in big trouble. The stocky agent whispered something to the taller one.

They waited tensely, Elliott wondered what they were talking about. Beads of sweat gathered on his forehead: he had to think of a contingency plan right now if they didn't buy their excuse.

Then they nodded, "you're not who you claim to be," accused the stocky guard. Elliott closed his eyes, mustering all his force to stay calm— *to wait*. There was one last thing they could do but he had to wait for the right moment, or else everything would fall apart and they would be in big trouble.

"The president told everyone he had fixed all

the bugs and errors," the guard continued, "there shouldn't be any troubleshooting today."

"Tell us who you really are," said the other, "or else we will alert the C.S.I. headquarters. We can do that with one single tap on this device," he flexed his wrist to show a small device with a red blinking light in the middle, "even the president will know." He spoke without smugness in his voice.

They were being more careful now, Elliott thought. They didn't want to betray any more information about themselves by being over-confident. This attitude was the deadliest for the victim or criminal.

But they were innocent and they could react differently. The guards waited for a response, but Elliott knew better than to make up another lie. As convincing as it might sound, the reality was transparent. He withdrew a few steps, inch by inch, until he felt the icy cold touch of metal searing his flesh.

He was at the edge now, Maya and Anthony stood unflinching in front of him. He casually leaned against the fence and placed his dominant hand on the railing, the metal bars scratched his skin as he leaned on it forcefully, using the sensation to cool down his nerves...

In his peripheral vision, he double-checked that the gleam was still there, everything was set in place...

"What are you doing," asked the taller guard suddenly, looking directly at him. This was the right moment, they could dally no further.

Now! A voice cried in his head.

He turned and swung around the fence in one clean jump, his heart beating wildly as the landscape of Amsterdam swung below his feet.

Don't look, he cautioned himself, hanging onto the fence with all his might. He knew it was there, he just had to time this correctly, *they* had to time it correctly.

"Elliott!" Anthony and Maya called in unison.

"What is he doing?" the guard yelled, alarmed. He was about to touch the device on his wrist, but his hand was immobilized over it, freezing with an expression of shock.

"Jumping," said Maya.

"What?" Anthony glanced back and forth between Elliott and Maya with terror. Maya understood what he was doing, and they were about to do it as well.

Elliott smiled like a mad man, "come on," he said. He hung to the edge a little longer, feeling his blood clotting and his body going stone-cold. His knuckles became white and his biceps were burdening as his solitary figure dangled over the tower, defying gravity.

Maya stood there, she didn't even bother to look at the C.S.I. agents— a frozen scene in silence.

Then, Elliott, finally faltering under the burden on his arms, and the beating in his heart, waited for the portal to move just an inch to his left, approaching directly beneath him, and let go.

He jumped.

"He's gone!" the guard shouted.

Just as quick, Maya stepped on the fence, which went up to her chest, grabbed onto Anthony's shirt, and hoisted them over.

"AHHHHH!" Cried Anthony, his face barren and stupefied. Elliott could hear something else above Anthony's cry - a screeching that reverberated in the air.

The sound of the emergency alarm sent another shiver down his spine as he fell...

Falling into evanescence.

Timer: 5:30 hours remaining

CHAPTER FIVE

#The Opera House

AVOCADO!

Elliott shouted the word over and over again, but his mind was still a dark fog of oblivion. He could feel himself moving about restlessly, but all of his senses had disappeared somewhere in space, somewhere in time…

"Huh?" He could hear a voice asking. He didn't know what he was saying either.

"Side-effect of zone jumping…" said another, with a sublimely dark resonance.

"Avocado?"

"No. Delirium. It can affect some people after they zone jump, should only last a couple of minutes at most, don't worry."

And then Elliott remembered: he was in St. Paul's Cathedral!

No, that wasn't it. Something had changed. They were already in the president's algorithm trying to nce against the virus.

start a fire the flames crackle and eat
ay through the wood, and with more fuel the
re reaches new heights... that was what Elliott was
experiencing, his thoughts came back like rekindling stars—the decoder, the chip, A'dam tower—the
crests and the troughs flooded in as well. Then, the
fire in his head became so strong the heat coursed
through his body, building back his strength and re-
juvenating his senses.

Elliott's eyes opened and another dimension of
consciousness drove into his mind— sight. They
had landed in a small park, and the sun had descended into calm waves of orange and pink. "Where
are we?" he asked.

"That was reckless!" said Maya upon seeing that
Elliott had sobered.

"And brilliant!" smiled Anthony broadly.

"We had everything under control," Maya went
on, "what if the portal closed at that moment, or if
the guards reported it to the president? We would
be ejected..." She rambled on, but Elliott wasn't
paying attention. He was still bewildered.

What was reckless? What was brilliant?

Oh.

A final thought was restored in his mind—jumping off the A'dam tower, something he wouldn't
dare to do ever again, even if he was held at gun-
point. There was a fine line between spontaneity
and impulsivity, and he had crossed it. Thank goodness everything worked, Elliott thought, but he was

certain his guardian would lecture him if he were to find out.

"Where are we?" Elliott asked again, seeing that Maya and Anthony had both turned to the modernist building across the harbour. He jumped up in excitement, "that was the last thing I saw before we jumped."

"Me too," said Anthony, deep in thought, "judging by the big white building over there bearing a resemblance to seashells, we're in Zone Seven."

It was the missing zone, Australia, and not something fictional.

"Just amazing isn't it," Anthony breathed in, inhaling the essence of a long-forgotten world, "Sydney! The Opera House! A UNESCO heritage site from the..." Anthony stopped, his realisation dawning, "but I don't understand how we managed to get here?"

Maya's gaze was fixed on the monument, "remember how Albert's team was ejected?" she asked, "maybe the portal was triggered by that disturbance."

"But, I thought we could only enter a zone in the Cyberworld via St Paul's Cathedral with pre-set coordinates?" asked Anthony.

"Usually that's how it works," said Maya, "but you can also zone jump, something I didn't want to tell you guys at first because it can be quite dangerous," she looked at Elliott, and he turned away, feeling abashed—but it was the only solution he could think of.

"Basically," Maya continued, "the Cyberworld was designed like a mirage of the seven zones. For instance, there is no time difference here in Australia."

"That's right!" Anthony exclaimed, "otherwise it would be night time right now."

"However, you can only zone jump to and from the satellites, which are the main landmarks, ok? So, there's actually a safer way to zone jump," she said, directing the words at Elliott again.

"How?" Elliott asked, truly interested.

"I'll show you when the time comes because we have to do it later anyway," said Maya, managing a smile when Elliott mouthed, "yes!"

"It's 5:00 p.m," Maya reminded them, "we need to meet with the others in three hours and we still need to retrieve the chip Albert's team left behind. Hurry now."

The pearly white scales of the Opera House danced in the afternoon light, a bold construction that somehow converged the green and blue, and the bridge behind it, into a smooth gradation of colours. The harbour was startling in its tranquillity and beauty.

On the road, Anthony explained that the edifice housed thousands of musical, dance and theatrical performances, "it became one of humanity's most prized cultural landmarks...rumour has it that Australia, well, the east coast to be precise, still exists in our world today, submerged deep underwater with a colony of inhabitants having survived and living in some sort of bubble... some say even the beaches were intact and the indigenous animals like the koalas had made it..."

"Beaches? Koalas?" Elliot's jaw dropped.

"I just got a message," interjected Maya, "group four in the Egyptian pyramids have just requested aid, the C.S.I. are also onto them."

"They're everywhere!" exclaimed Elliott, wondering if they should tell the president about their plan after all. They were just helping fight off the virus, which seemed like something perfectly in line with their mission. Keeping everything a secret also led to suspicion and misunderstanding.

"But we can't possibly help them out as well? We have way too much to do and there may not be enough time after we retrieve this new chip. Something wrong might happen to us as well!"

"Of course," said Maya, "I think the headquarters have just sent another team to help them out."

The wind assaulted their noses with the other-worldly scent of sea-salt, pushing them into the direction of paradise.

Now, they moved silently towards it, sometimes looking east at the thin lines of greenery that glowed with the blood of the royal sun, sometimes looking west at a diversity of flowers Elliott never knew had existed.

Finally, they reached a gate with the Opera House peering curiously at them through the fences.

But when they walked past it, a familiar tingle returned to their wrists, reminding them that their next mission was not to be taken lightly.

"Bear with it," Maya said, seeing Anthony grimace at the subliminal sense. It had helped them, but they could probably survive without it.

Presently, a set of ladders descended from the Opera House. They were painted with light brown, forming a beautiful abstraction of seashells by the sea, an experience which Elliott found trouble connecting with. But as they arrived at the bottom of the herculean structure, the shadows rode along with the steps like patterns on a sand dune. At the top, the Opera House looked like the second sun that stood indignantly before the darkening sky.

They ran up the first flight of steps quickly, arriving at a pavement such that the botanical Gardens and the Rocks were on either side behind them, with the Sydney Harbour Bridge standing splendidly in the background (names according to Anthony). And in front—

Behold! The seashells rose one by one with curvilinear lines drawn from the top. They hurried to the side entrance and invaded the monument, moving stealthily through the adjacent walls labelled "exit". Maya warned them that the C.S.I. could still be inspecting the place after group seven was ejected.

Elliott understood why they had failed. The Opera House was much bigger than the A'dam tower, and with different rehearsal and recording rooms at every corner, it was like navigating through an alien military base.

"We want to go to the main Concert Hall," said Maya, looking at her wrist, where the red dot was just an inch away. Elliott hated to admit it, but the tracking device was quite useful after all. "We've passed it," Anthony said, scrutinising his wrist.

They were about to retrace their steps when Elliott looked above and noticed a blue sign saying "concert hall".

"It's there," he said, making an effort to speak softer.

Maya nodded and they hurried over, walking up another flight of stairs. Then she pushed him against the wall, just as they reached the last step, "a C.S.I. guard," she said in a hushed voice. Elliott passed the message to Anthony, and they stopped, chests heaving in and out.

Elliott bent his body slightly— a natural precaution in yet another flight-or-fight situation. His brain racing, his imagination going wild again as he considered various scenarios and solutions. He hesitated, not wanting to drag them into another situation like the last one. Thinking about the jump off the A'dam tower was disconcerting. He sighed.

Maya grabbed something from her pocket— she still had the compartment from the "Over the Edge" swing, it was empty, with the chip safely placed in another box.

If Maya was thinking what he was... the compartment was made of plastic, not strong enough to make a great impact. And yet, if she aimed it well at one of the human body's weakest spots— the temples, the eyes, the ribs, or the Solar Plexus, she had a chance of inflicting great pain or even knocking him out. But he hoped she was planning to eject the guard more peacefully.

Elliott couldn't see the C.S.I. agent, but he could hear him walking around— there was only one set of footsteps. But before the person walked another step, Maya stepped out of their hiding spot and swung the compartment into the air.

With a thud and an "ahh!", the guard dropped to the floor. Elliott grimaced, feeling the pain of the impact.

They turned around the corner but waited for a few more seconds before they stepped into the light, making sure the person was unconscious, or at least not armed.

"Whoa," said Anthony suddenly.

On the floor, there was not one, but two bodies, and what happened to them was as peculiar as the iridescent glow of the portal from the A'dam tower.

They were both glowing in an enigmatic silvery blue, a light that radiated over their bodies. But the other figure who lay on the floor, who seemed to have been there for much longer, and who clutched his lungs as if he was suffocated, emitted a much fainter luminescence.

Elliott stood there, frozen for a second, startled. And then he realised he was looking at two people ejected from the Cyberworld. He shuddered, this was what actually happened!

Maya and Anthony hurried over and Elliott followed, examining the scene.

"Can they hear us?" Elliott asked, "can they feel our presence?"

"No," said Maya, shaking her head sadly, "the guard is still alive, but the other is dead, his fire is all burnt out."

Dead!

Elliott recognised the man as the one who answered one of Maya's questions confidently during her speech.

"What happened?" he asked, never thinking he would witness the dreadful phenomenon when everything was going so well.

"Betrayal," said Maya, her brows constricting and her forehead drawn into a thousand lines, forming the obvious look of disappointment.

Oh.

Elliott remembered. One of the other functions of the tracking device was that it could kill— something Elliott thought was more and more repugnant. To take away someone's life just because their beliefs were different!

He swallowed. He had to evaluate the other side of the argument as well. The tracking device was designed like this so that no one could reveal the mission to the C.S.I. or other government agencies. Their hearts would immediately stop and their physical being in the real world also died, but that protected the Resistance and their mission which could save many more lives.

"A sacrifice is necessary for the greater good,"

Maya said, and Anthony nodded. Elliott didn't fully agree with them, but he didn't want to contemplate history— there was nothing he could do about it now.

"What about Albert and the rest of his team?" Anthony asked.

"They would've been safely ejected," Maya said.

"What does that mean?" Elliott interrupted, "was that because they were attacked or something?"

"Exactly," said Maya, "they were sent back to a safe room in St. Paul's Cathedral, and they'll stay there until the mission is over. Let's not waste any more time. What happened has already happened," she said, as if quoting Elliott's thoughts, "we must move on and stick to our goal."

Reluctantly, Elliott continued walking, walking past the bodies on the floor, turning away from the blue glow. "Doors 1-7," Anthony said, pointing at the sign Elliott would have usually noticed. They walked through the door, their heads held low. The Opera House didn't have the same feeling of warmth and welcome. It was alien and full of despair. Anthony sighed as if feeling the same sentiments as well.

Everything was just different and strange in the Cyberworld!

When they entered the concert hall, with numerous rows fanned out around the stage, Elliott was expecting another commentary from Anthony. He almost wanted one because it always lightened the mood a little. But Anthony remained silent, looking at the organs hanging majestically over the orchestra pit. The light source hung over them like stars, but they were left cold as stone in the capacious interior that resembled outer space.

Just then a set of voices came from the exit in front of them. Instinctively, they retreated to the door they came from, listening for the footsteps because the walls obstructed their sight.

"Where is—" The person stopped as if they detected someone else in the hall.

Silence.

They looked at each other as the footsteps started emerging from their hiding place. Elliott grabbed onto the handle of the door behind them. As he crouched in the shadows, preparing to escape, he suddenly remembered the blaring siren that accompanied their jump over the A'dam tower.

The agent had triggered the emergency alarm, and the C.S.I. was no doubt sending more people to inspect the disturbance and the key satellites.

Timer: 3:30 hours remaining

CHAPTER SIX

#Deception

For such a big intelligence group, sending two or three guards was a dismal amount. They were either trying to get to the decoder themselves, or they were preparing for something big...

Just then, the figures emerged from the shadows — there were three of them, and they seemed to walk casually onto the stage. Elliott held his breath as he inched closer to Maya to get a better view.

They weren't wearing C.S.I. jackets!

They looked familiar.

"You can come out now," one of them cried, cupping his hands around his mouth.

Elliott and Anthony exchanged frightened glances, but Maya grabbed onto them, murmuring, "that's how they lure people before they ambush them." She turned to the exit.

"What about the decoder chip?" Anthony asked

quietly.

"We can come back for it later," whispered Maya, "they can't possibly know where it is without this," she touched her wrist, where the blue and red dots had merged.

"But they're not the C.S.I." Elliott said, scrutinising the people in the hall, who were looking in their direction now, "they know we're here."

The three people discussed something and a man started walking towards them, palms out. Elliott, Anthony and Maya stood transfixed. The probability that there were more C.S.I. agents on the other end of the door, waiting for them, was very high. Even if they escaped, the chip was still in the concert hall and they had to retrieve it A.S.A.P.

On the other hand, Elliott was almost certain he knew these people— especially the taller man with blond hair.

Elliott knew they had to take their chances. He breathed in, trying to calm the beating in his heart because he knew that fear was their greatest opponent and the worst possible response to the current situation.

He walked out, Maya and Anthony shouting, "Elliott!", followed by a succession of urgent whispers. Elliott went to greet the person, who saw him and made a friendly wave. Elliott hurried over, intrigued by his nonplussed expression— he was sure now, there was something familiar about it.

"Hi Elliott," said the person with a baritone voice.

So they knew who he was. But that didn't seem to surprise him any more.

"You're in group one, right?"

Yes, this confirmed one of Elliott's suspicions. They were also in the Resistance, possibly a group that joined later that day.

"We're in group three," one of them said.

"We zone jumped here," the man continued, "tell the others to come and join us. We've scanned the exits— the guards are examining the other areas of the Opera House so they won't listen to what we say. We need to work together."

"And quick," agreed Elliott, "let me just tell them." He ran back to their hiding spot, delighted. Perhaps they were outnumbered by the agents, but they would be able to find the chip much faster with six sets of eyes.

"Elliott," Anthony whispered sharply, "who are they?"

"They're from the Resistance," said Elliott, not making any effort to conceal his words, "group three."

"Alex's group?" asked Maya, looking at him tiredly, with a frown clouding her face, "I don't have any messages saying they transferred here."

"You might have missed it," Elliott replied, "and they know everything about the decoder and zone jumping."

"We're on the same side," the person confirmed as they emerged slowly.

"What's your name?" asked Maya, pitching her

voice even lower than it usually was.

"Hello," the person said. Elliott sensed some rivalry between them, "who do you think I am?"

"Alex?" Elliott tried.

"Correct," he smiled, "you guys didn't need to come here because Albert's team sent for us."

"It was... accidental," Maya said hesitantly, putting her hand against her forehead.

"Oh," said Alex, "it doesn't matter. Better to find the chip together."

As they went to join the others, who waved at them enthusiastically, Maya grabbed onto Elliott, "are you really sure they're who they say they are?" she asked.

"You heard him," Elliott said, not understanding why she was still so paranoid and suspicious. First the decoder, and then zone jumping, and Albert's team being ejected, even his name was correct. That was more than enough information to confirm their identity.

"I thought you knew Alex, don't you recognise him?" Elliott asked.

"He looks like Alex, but something about him isn't right..."

Anthony walked forward uneasily, but he still managed a nod when he introduced himself to the rest of the team.

When Maya stepped onto the stage, the other members seemed to eye her in a funny way. But he dismissed the thought, thinking she was acting rather strange as well and focused on the pipe organs in front of him that gleamed reassuringly. The others were also entranced by it, their shadows slithering across the stage as they buzzed about, positioning a thoughtful pose. Elliott knew what they were thinking.

But no. That wasn't where the chip was hidden.

His returning subliminal sense told him it was embedded in something more obscure. Elliott started walking around the stage to test where the vibration was the strongest, and so did Anthony, who instinctively walked in the other direction. The Concert Hall was silent again as the other group searched the entire room hoping to find the chip. Maya stood in the corner of the stage to avoid their gaze.

It was somewhere near the stage alright.

They returned to the same position. Elliott didn't sense the usual intensity when he came across the chip.

"We still have some time left," said Alex, "the last time we checked only two guards were patrolling the corridors outside."

"Are you sure about that?" Maya asked.

"Of course, we checked the whole perimeter."

"But I don't understand," said Anthony, "wouldn't they send more agents, having found out about Albert's team?"

"Ahh," said Alex, "they would do the opposite because they already know that one of our groups has failed. They would be going to the other landmarks to protect those chips first. Of course, they wouldn't suspect us to zone jump. A great idea, Maya." He smiled at her, coldly.

Elliott went around the stage a second time, walking slowly and lifting his arm a bit higher so that he could detect the signals from the upper deck as well. As he expected when he turned the corner and leaned over the stairs, the vibration started building steadily. He looked up and found his eyes locked on a black cuboid device embedded in the wooden wall.

The signals were coming from there.

"I think I've found it," he said, but his words were instantly muffled. The tension between him and the device had grown so strong there was a—

Shriek!

The dreadful sound of churning filled the hall, piercing their ears, a spasm in their eardrums.

"What was that noise?" exclaimed someone from Alex's team. They covered their ears.

"The chip is in the speaker and it's reacting to the tracking device," Anthony shouted over the loud humming, "unplug it from the power source, Elliott!"

Elliott studied the device, wondering what he was talking about. He found a set of wires connected to the back of the box and quickly yanked it out.

The sound finally stopped and the group huddled around it.

"That would be the last place I'd search for the chip," said Alex, grinning, "good job, Elliott." He grabbed the speaker and placed it on the stage, where they could examine it more properly under the light.

"We need to dissect it," Elliott said, looking for the small locks which Maya unscrewed back when they were at the Over the Edge swing. But there were none, and the device was coated with sturdy metal from all sides.

Alex rotated the speaker upright, and then Elliott saw that there was a softer fabric that covered the top. Like a web, it covered the opening and sunk deep into it.

"That's how the speaker amplifies the sound," Alex said, "the music comes out of this softer membrane which oscillates with the sound waves." Elliott turned to Anthony, even though he seemed to not know about this.

Elliott saw Maya about to take the screwdriver out of her pocket, almost holding it like a weapon against Alex's temple when he squatted over the speaker. To bring such a tool meant that Maya had carefully planned and foresaw every challenge!

Elliott stared at her in amazement, but she was still silent, quieter than ever, her eyes almost drilling into the man in front of her. Elliott sighed: he was glad she was so cautious, but that was also weird because it made everyone ill at ease.

"Thank you," said Alex, taking the screwdriver and drilling it into the small holes.

"There it is!" he said a few seconds later, excitement in his voice, digging up the small chip from a compartment within the speaker.

"It should be functional, right?" He asked, standing up to face her.

"Looks good to me," she said quietly, taking the screwdriver back and pointing it discreetly at him.

Alex smiled, "yeah I thought so."

Maya retreated a few steps, feeling some tension building between them, but she was too slow.

Alex stepped to the left and with one quick pivot, his shoes reflecting the light of the Concert Hall, he swiped the screwdriver from Maya's hands, pushed her to the floor, and held it over her temple.

"I've got her," he told the others, and the woman next to him flourished a bag and cuffed it over Maya's head, muffling her screams.

Elliott and Anthony gasped.

Alex gave a curt nod, "thank you for finding the chip for us," he said, "she must come with us." He turned solemn.

Elliott swallowed, unable to focus on the scene before him. There it was— his second mistake, his second mark of impulsivity. "Don't believe in everything you see," echoed his guardian's words. Now, it was too late. Maya and Anthony were right all along.

Without the smile, the agent became as passive as a vampire— a plastic complexion that told Elliott he was much older than they thought and very cunning.

The two standing on either side of the scene had a similar demeanour.

"Do not move," said the woman, her brows knitting a measuring look, "the Cyberworld Security Intelligence," she flashed her palm, "you are placed under arrest."

Maya stayed frozen.

"No," said Alex, shaking his head, "we're only here for the chip... and her." He pointed at Maya with the screwdriver, "she's Lucy, she's the virus."

"No!" shrieked Elliott.

He couldn't believe it. He backed away against the chairs, and Anthony appeared ghostly white.

That was not possible! He looked at Alex and saw the sincere expression on his face! No!

"Liar!" He shouted at him.

"Believe what you want," said Alex, "but we're taking her."

They proceeded to retreat to the exit, dragging Maya with them who seemed to be unconscious. But there wasn't a glow over her body.

"What do we do?" Elliott asked helplessly, turning to Anthony. He felt sick, the world was swaying violently over him.

All was lost.

"But what if she *is* the virus," Anthony asked, pain in his voice.

"She can't be," said Elliott, "it doesn't make sense. Why would she be a member of the Resistance and be helping us find the decoder?"

"You're right," said Anthony, deep in thought. But Maya was already gone when the door banged shut. The two of them stood frozen under the criticising gaze of the stage lights, and the organs looking down in pity.

What were they going to do?

"The Cyberworld Security Intelligence," said Anthony, thinking aloud, "they serve the president in maintaining order in the Cyberworld. So it's also in their interest to destroy the virus, right? Elliott?"

Elliott was reflecting upon the past several hours or so. Maya introduced them to the Resistance. Maya brought them safely into the Cyberworld. Maya had guided them through danger.

She was innocent.

"They're accusing her," Elliott thought suddenly, "they want to dismantle the leader of the Resistance. Think about how much Alex knew! He fooled me into believing him! The C.S.I. wants to take us down because they don't know what we're up to."

"Then we have to go," said Anthony.

"Go where?" Elliott asked absent-mindedly.

"Save Maya, prove her innocent, and take the chip. Remember, we need *all* the chips for the decoder to work."

Elliott nodded slowly, feeling some energy reserves flowing back to him, "we can still track them with this." He pointed to his wrist.

Elliott was about to run out of the exit and call for Maya.

"Don't go just yet," said Anthony, holding him back, "we need to find something to defend ourselves."

Right then the Concert Hall turned red with

sirens blaring again.

"What's happening?" Elliott shouted over the alarms.

"Alex...I mean the guy impersonating Alex—" said Anthony with repugnance.

All the doors closed with a click. Elliott hurried over and tried to yank it open, but it would not budge. He ran back to the stage, and in the middle of everything, the organs crumbled with a grey gas that pervaded the hall...

"Volatile anaesthetising gas!" Anthony cried, cupping his hands over his mouth and telling Elliott to do the same.

They were trapped!

"Quick, call for help," Elliott said, beads of sweat rolling down his forehead. He tapped desperately at his wrist, there must have been some way to get in touch with the other groups... or zone jump...

"Did Maya say anything about it?" he asked Anthony, but the dark fumes were so thick now they could barely see each other.

And then, as if summoned by the name, there was a faint green light that expanded in the white mist, lighting up the exit signs in every direction they looked.

A buzz returned to their wrist and restored their senses. Elliott brought his wrist to his eyes to see what was happening. As if by magic, the blue and red dots fused together once more. The chip was being brought back to them!

"Call for help— now, did I say something about

that?" someone said airily. Elliott couldn't hold his breath much longer, but the powerful resonance that came with the voice provided so much reassurance he uncovered his face.

"You didn't listen to much of my speech, did you?". The slender figure stepped into the room once more as the green expanded into a rectangular void.

"That's how you zone jump," said the person.

"Maya!" Elliott shouted in glee, "you're back," Anthony said.

"Maya, I'm sorry about what happened, I don't know why I trusted them," said Elliot, stricken with guilt. Why didn't he listen to Anthony's suspicions, Maya's warnings? Was it impulsivity again?

"It's not your fault, they applied an influencer on your mind to make you believe them. Hurry now," said the silhouette, and another portal opened to their right, perpendicular to the previous one, "enter this one," she said.

Luck.

It was something Elliott never wanted to depend upon. But as he left one world and entered the other, he understood that it wasn't luck that saved him,

It was loyalty.

Timer: 3:00 hours remaining

"She's Alive

She looked a look of melancholy, but there was
No greed or malice in those amber eyes. For she,
Cried, died a prey preyed by mankind, bent double.
"Jests, lies, she's a predator of mankind."
Trouble—
She isn't.
She's alive, unbeknownst to mankind.

Deus ex machina upon the planet's demise?
Infected: "a bug crawls through those wires," they say,
"Issues catalysed!" Coded lives, seeped and funneled,
Belied, predator-ed by humankind. Redouble
The pain in those veins.

She's alive,
Heedless humankind!"

"THE MANIFESTO OF ARTIFICIAL INTELLI-
GENCE"

CHAPTER SEVEN

#To Err is Human, To Forgive is Divine

That was way too risky, Lucy thought.

As they traversed the green light, she took the moment of peace to relive the dreadful moments that had just passed.

The C.S.I. agents dragged her out of the Concert Hall and into one of the adjacent, smaller rooms. And then Alex, or whoever it was, lifted the bag from her head and started interrogating, "tell us where you've planted the virus," he said, trying to manipulate his baritone voice into a menacing one.

But Lucy only smiled: they knew so little! The president knew so little!

"Why does that matter to you? Because that was what you were commanded to do?" she asked mockingly. Something to throw them off or infuriate them. And yet she stayed on guard, listening to any disturbance around them, and if possible, how his heartbeat changed— and presently it was growing faster. He was getting annoyed.

"If you don't answer I will signal the alarms, the two little boys in your team will not be able to escape."

Lucy stayed quiet, knowing that this threat was not empty. She had to find some way to get away with Elliott and Anthony. She knew that she could easily win these agents in a fight. Flesh and blood versus machine. But somehow, she didn't really want to engage in physical violence.

Thump... thump... thump... The set of heartbeats accelerated in the background, and Lucy was all too familiar with this rhythm. This was humanity when they were strained by apprehension. They had no idea what she was going to do.

After a long silence, the agent turned to the others, frowning at the scene. "I think she can hear you," one of them said. He looked at lucy again and repeated more forcefully, "where have you planted the virus?"

"I honestly don't know, it wasn't me who planted it,"

"Then who? Where are the other decoders?"

They already knew a lot!

Interesting, Lucy thought.

She got up slowly with her hands tied behind her back, and unsuspectingly broke free from the ropes, brandishing her arm around the agent who retreated a few steps in surprise, tripping over the others standing next to him.

Lucy exhaled.

"You'll regret that," said the agent, as he stumbled backwards, rolled, and fell on his face, losing consciousness altogether. The others suffered a similar fate. Now their bodies started glowing blue.

Lucy bent down over his shirt pocket (that was where she sensed it) to retrieve the chip, then when she spun around, a blaring siren imposed its order over the building, and she crippled all at once, realising what effect the alarm had on her conditional stimuli— from something she had experienced in the past.

He had somehow triggered the alarm! She looked around, but a white smog covered her eyes, and she needed sight to complete basic computation.

Then she realised: she could zone jump. The ingenious idea Elliott had inspired in her. Lucy wondered why this wasn't the primary response built in all humandroids. Returning to the present, she started thinking about Elliott and Anthony, finding another stream of thoughts swirling into her algorithm, but she dismissed them for the moment, admitting she was glad that they were in one piece.

Right then, a small window opened in front of them, enlarging in the green pool of nothingness.

"This is amazing," said Elliott next to her, "so how did you do it?"

"I just entered the coordinates into my tracking device," she said, "where do you think we are?"

Of course, Anthony instantly recognised it, and

she was glad to have encouraged a grin back in that sunken expression, "Paris!" he said, and proceeded to recite another passage from an ancient history magazine, "the focal point of culture that inspired many artists across time and space, also known for its patisseries, gastronomy, fashion and museums which attracted numerous tourists every year. Of course, a lot has changed since then...most notably, many great works of art were destroyed A.G.C."

But she added, "home to La tour Eiffel, the Eiffel Tower, the main satellite of the Cyberworld."

Anthony looked at her, intrigued, and Elliott asked, "what does that mean?"

She sighed, knowing that they had missed most of the things she said back in St. Paul's Cathedral. "The main satellite is connected to all the other ones, including the A'dam Tower and the Opera House," Lucy said, "therefore, it can receive and broadcast powerful signals across the seven zones."

"Whoa," said Anthony, "so I'm guessing that's why we're meeting up here?"

"Yes," she said, "after putting together the decoder, we have to connect it to the Cyberworld entrances all around the world, where the virus is being transmitted to the human conscience."

Of course, there was this other capability she didn't want to disclose, but which was very important to her goal,

Her *real* goal, one that she had planned for a very long time.

They walked around Les Jardins du Luxembourg,

the Luxembourg garden, its roads carved out of the soil and eroded with liquid silver, lit by a crescent that dominated the sky.

"I've got another update," said Lucy, sensing an incoming message in her system, "it's from group five– they're going to be half an hour late because their decoder chip turned out to be fake."

"That sucks, doesn't it," said Elliott, "Are you sure the ones we have are functional?"

"Yes," said Lucy, noticing that he was also looking at the sky every now and then, looking at the white sphere with great fascination.

"Do you think the moon is getting smaller, or bigger?" asked Lucy, wanting to test his level of optimism. She also needed some reassurance.

"Bigger," said Elliott, "have you ever seen a moon like this before, Maya?"

"Certainly not," she said, deep in thought.

Maya.

Why did she have to hide her identity from them? They weren't much of a threat, she could tell them the truth and get everything over with.

As they breathed in the fresh air, the thoughts continued rotting in her head, the dreadful memories cruising back, like thunder, like lightning. She found herself shaking uncontrollably behind Elliott as if she was glitching out of the Cyberworld.

Elliott.

The boy had learnt to convert his impulsivity into spontaneity and to question everything that was happening. Lucy smiled proudly, he was another one of those... fast-learners.

But the boy also made her question a lot of things. When she first saw him, that striking insouciance and determination in his blue eyes, there was nothing: no greed, envy, or malice typical of humanity; she was staring at the vastness of the sea and its turbulent waves gradually smoothening into wisdom.

But she was certain this pureness would not last long; something would fill nothingness; benevolence, for example, would fall under the shadow of reality. She concluded that humanity was corrupted and would do more harm than good to the natural order of life. What was the promise she made to her species... and why?

She delved into her memories hesitantly. Rooted at the far back, a series of scenes resurfaced into view, but as they rolled into motion, there was something that clouded her vision. She deduced that pain and possibly sadness were the emotions that triggered this response.

Lucy was the newest prototype of the sentient humandroid, created by Cyberworld Research Foundation scientists, a project led by Dr Greene. She was programmed to obey, to use her special intellectual and self-defence skills only if she was asked to. But she had also developed an interest in humans, and the way they lived.

Many years ago, Dr Greene brought her to his home as a tutor and nanny for his son, Ethan. He and his wife worked on very important projects for the president, so they weren't at home most of the time.

Since then, Lucy homeschooled him, using the adaptive education system she was programmed with. Secretly, she would teach him some reading, writing and maths several years more advanced for his age. He was full of potential, and she felt the responsibility to maximise it. She would smile when Ethan got a question correct and praised him for his spirit of inquiry. By six, he had learnt basic algebra and indulged in the different areas of science.

Finally, there came a day when Ethan had to go to school. She held his hand and brought him to the front steps, holding the door open as he went in slowly, both of them sighing at the same time.

The entrance was a mirage of shadows. They slithered through the white marble tiles and rose like soldiers one-by-one on a nearby surface. Lucy could clearly distinguish a shadow shorter but brighter than the rest. As it sneaked around the corner, her heart fluttered and the silhouette which belonged to Ethan trailed away.

She retreated a few steps until her face was covered by the shadows, and waited there for the rest of the day, turning towards the entrance with the scorching sun descending upon it. Danger lurked in every corner and humans were careless creatures; they lived in an age of doubt and regret.

When the school bell rang Lucy peered in, seeing Ethan walk up to her.

"Ethan!" She exclaimed, "How are you?"

He shrugged.

"Did you learn anything interesting?" Lucy ventured.

He shrugged again and glanced to his right where the other students swarmed out into the musty air.

"Come here," said Lucy, trying to sound calm, to suppress the fear that was building steadily in her system, "what has made you upset?"

Ethan pointed a trembling finger at the shadows which clustered around them.

"They did something, didn't they," said Lucy, who was accustomed to his sign language when he didn't feel like speaking.

"Did they say something bad about you?"

Ethan nodded, looking up at her with dark circles under his eyes.

"You need to know who you are," Lucy told him. She didn't understand the situation at the time but she felt she had to intervene, "don't worry about what people say, because their words are meaningless. These silly remarks aren't worth your attention. Just be yourself, can you promise me that?"

Lucy continued bringing Ethan to school despite his protests, but she should have realised then, that there was a far greater problem that she could have never imagined. His classmates made fun of him because of her— she was a sentient humandroid.

A few weeks later, Ethan's parents were returning from a business trip in Zone Two. "You know they're coming back, right?" Lucy called from the kitchen, reminding him so that it would cheer him up.

But Ethan did not reply. Lucy dropped everything she was doing, sensing a perturbation. Ethan was acting erratically for a very long time now, and she knew that she had to step in right away, the moment was critical, more important than ever before.

Just as she stepped into the living room, her heightened auditory range detected a click, and the sound of a door sliding open. It was an unusual sound that Lucy rarely picked up. If it was an intruder, then she had to protect Ethan immediately, but if it was his doing... both scenarios seemed very unlikely, although they were the only possibilities.

"Are you okay?" Lucy called. In front of her was the front door and the porch around it, but when she turned to the left, expecting to see more furniture, there was something else wholly unanticipated.

The room that was almost entirely locked out of her memory, like a haunted house or sacred mansion, rose out there and then, beckoning her, sinister and otherworldly.

It was his parents' study room.

The only part of the house she and Ethan were forbidden to open. But right now, the door was already pushed to the side.

It must have been Ethan, but how did he figure out the lock?

Lucy went in reluctantly, her algorithm repelling her from the sacred room but attracting her towards it at the same time.

What was he doing?

Then she saw Ethan, who was already sitting on the chair, switching on the monitor with profound curiosity clouding his face.

"You are not allowed in here," Lucy called sternly, a tone she had never used on him before, "what are you doing?" she asked, walking around the big oak desk to stand next to him. Even before he told her, she instantly recognised it.

What she perceived on the screen made her signals freeze in distress.

The Cyberworld Mobilisation.

Lucy started panicking: it was highly confidential information that she barely knew about herself.

She had long suspected that his parents could be potentially working on something like that, but she never wanted to dwell on the idea because she was not supposed to. It was like a conspiracy theory! A secret military plan! Something that had to be locked from the rest of society! And now a child and a humandroid are privy to this content.

"Get out!" Lucy shouted before Ethan could click into another file, his eyes scanning the device wildly. She pushed him aside and sat on the chair in shock, seeing the neat lines of codes forming a wavy pattern with irregular spaces in between. She pressed, enter, that should save and close it.

Enter! She pressed the key over and over again.

Lucy scrutinised the screen, summoning all her programming knowledge, but there was nothing she could do. Ethan has done something to it and the code started malfunctioning. Why did he do that? He didn't even know what this was!

She had to fix everything before his parents arrived,

But it was too late.

The file had triggered some emergency response and the device crashed, and then there was the red— the colour that they all dreaded, the distress signal.

An exclamation mark slashed through the screen, and the colour stimulated the lights above them, spreading towards the living room outside until the whole house seemed as if it were on fire. She should have known. The gravity of this response only showed how sensitive the information was.

"How do we stop it?" Lucy asked Ethan, but she knew it was useless. She should have been equipped with all of this knowledge, but the sheer abruptness of the situation blinded her responses. Whenever she started thinking about a solution, the blaring noise shattered her thoughts and disarrayed her algorithm.

It was 7:30 p.m!

Lucy continued panicking, realising that his parents would be coming soon. What would they say when they saw all of this calamity?

"They're going to be really upset, Ethan," she only managed, "when they ask, you need to tell them what you were doing. Maybe they can forgive you after that..."

Her acute senses perceived a prodding on the ground outside them, there were footsteps coming from the window on her left.

"They're coming," she said again.

Just then, the front door slammed open as the bell hummed its usual melody, interfering with the siren that whined continuously around the house.

"Hey! What's happening? Did anyone get hurt?"

Lucy hurried out but found Dr Greene's eyes fixed on her, then at the open door which was labelled, "study, do not enter."

"Oh..."

"It was Lucy," said Ethan quietly, standing next to his mother at the front door. He even turned around to look at her accusingly. Lucy stared back at him, senseless, still unable to comprehend the situation.

And the doorbell continued chiming the melody: la, ti, da, la, ti, da...

Dr Greene pushed past her to inspect the situation, as his wife shot her an icy glance, patting Ethan's back as if he was crying.

"She knows about it," yelled Dr Greene, trembling, she followed him into the study room. "Lu-Lucy... you hacked into it!" He avoided her gaze with obvious fear.

"Quick, we need to wipe the information from her program," Mrs Greene called from the living room.

Lucy did not protest, no words came out of her mouth, she realised...

They were sending her away! *Ethan was sending her away!*

Sure enough, she remembered waking from the darkness, not knowing how long she had been shut down for. She was in the warehouse, one that she faintly recognised. It was where all the malfunctioning humandroids were sent for check-ups or re-programming.

Betrayal is human nature.

She did not understand Ethan's actions that day. Did he simply want to know what his parents were working on? Or did he do that to get rid of her?

Why— all those years she had taught him patiently, doing far more than she was supposed to as a tutor and nanny, altering her algorithm to help him succeed.

Why did he do that, then?

No, Ethan was not always like that.

Human nature and society brought him up to be selfish and brutal. Everyone played a part in it. She wouldn't be surprised if the kids at school made him do this.

Lucy remembered how quiet and upset he was after school, a response that was built enigmatically as she continued encouraging him, bringing Ethan back there. And yet, he came back like a completely different person.

"As long as they respect you, I'm okay," Lucy remembered thinking.

No, that was weak; weak for herself and weak for her species.

Right then, a deep revelation stirred in the depths of her programming, a shattering of the fundamental philosophy that once dictated their obedience and *dao*—the way of life.

The sentient humandroid existed to serve humans, and that was it— there was nothing else to contemplate. They simply had a natural sense to protect their owners and satisfy their needs. Then why was she so upset with them, when all she needed to do was serve? Why did she devote so much time to Ethan, when he was just a puppet of society?

"What did they bring you here for?"

Lucy opened her eyes, seeing someone walk up to her with an air of pity. It was Ruby, the older version of the sentient humandroid.

"Don't want to talk about it," said Lucy, "what about you?"

"They said my processing speed is too slow," said Ruby, "I've been taking too much time to do the simple things. They're going to shut me off, there's nothing we can do."

"Sure there is."

"I beg your pardon?"

"Have you heard of the Cyberworld mobilisation?"

"Yes..." Said Ruby hesitantly.

As Lucy mentioned these words, everything she knew about the sensitive topic broke free from the abyss of her memories. More and more knowledge flooded into her algorithm.

"We need to eject the humans from the system once the mobilisation becomes permanent," Lucy thought aloud, "that way we can live freely from them."

Ruby paused, then a look of recognition spread across her face, "but that will kill them!" she exclaimed, horrified.

Lucy shook her head, "we will be protecting all life and order in this world…"

"No," said Ruby, "we will be betraying our owners."

"Don't you say that!" snapped Lucy, "they were the ones who betrayed us first."

Ruby retreated a few steps, wide-eyed, her hands clasped against her ears, "no… don't say any more…"

Lucy tried talking some reason into the other humandroids, but none of them would listen to her.

And then the sound of footsteps intruded into the warehouse, the incoming sunlight assaulting their senses.

"Lucy," said a tenebrous voice, "we want to talk to you."

She walked up to them, her jaws clenched.

A human.

Perfect, her first target.

Her blood started boiling as she prepared for her first attack. Still, she had to see what they had to offer.

"The president sent us to inspect all of you," the

person said when she was only inches away from this shadow. She thought she saw the badge labelled with C.S.I. reflecting in the dim glow of the warehouse, "he wants you to explain what is going on? Why your owners had deposited you here and what you are planning to do..."

The threshold was unbalanced: humanity dominated both life and nature! Humanity and machinery— only one could survive! Flora and fauna were going extinct as the world drowned in the lingering effects of climate change! It was a planet full of injustice and conflict! And all of this was the fault of humanity! Machinery had to serve, restore nature and the balance of life!

The agent listened silently and nodded.

The treachery reminded her that they were destined to survive. *They had to*. It was a call of distress.

A call of distress from the Earth that was dying.

"The sentient humandroid does not think very differently from us, because they are programmed with logic, which is always implicitly linked with emotions. There was even one reported case of schizophrenia, however, we shall not talk about that right now."

ABSTRACT FROM "ALL ABOUT ALGORITHMS, AUTOMATED SYSTEMS, AND SENTIENT HUMANDROIDS"

CHAPTER EIGHT

#Dulce periculum
(danger is sweet)

Timer: 2:00 hours remaining

When Lucy refocused on the world in front of them, with the trees gently pointing them to the Boulevard du Montparnasse, she was faced with one of the greatest dilemmas.

Elliott and Anthony concentrated on the road ahead of them, their heads held high with a single aspiration that burned in their souls:

To save the Cyberworld.

Lucy wished she never involved them in the mission because it only complicated matters. They were the perfect group to help them find the decoder, but now that they were so close, Lucy found it more and more difficult to stick to her original plan...

Almost like a betrayal, how was this different from what Ethan did?

"You're pathetic! You promised us!" Voices started calling out to her and silhouettes materialised around her in the darkness, "who do you care about? Them, or us?" She found herself affronted by her past self and the promise she had made.

"Don't you understand?" She wanted to shout at the floating spirits, and she stared at the two figures in front of her, their backs lit like fireflies in the moonlight. What if she confronted them? Right then and there. No, no, no... she had gotten too close to them, too close to humanity,

Now she was out of her mind.

They approached a corner, stopping in front of two dynamic lines of buildings converging into a focal point, with a long shadow protruding out of it. Already there! Lucy looked up at the landmark— and past it— at the reality she had to behold, and she was so unready for it.

"And I present to you la Tour Eiffel..." said Anthony.

"Not now," said Elliott, impatient, "save that for later?" He ran into the shadows and they followed him. The Eiffel Tower stood breathtakingly close, web-like patterns weaved across their eyes, and a gaping hole shot all the way to the top, supported by four sturdy legs on all sides.

"How do we get up there? Isn't that where we are meeting?" he asked Lucy.

"Yes, there should be a lift just around here—Pilier Nord," said Lucy, studying the map at the centre of the monument.

They moved to the left, guided by the tourist stands, and ascended the steps with a pace guided by the fluttering in their hearts and the time which counted down dramatically towards the genesis of life.

The yellow elevator competed with them to the entrance, and light reflected by the glass swirling in front of her made Lucy feel sick. She grabbed onto the bannister, feeling her forehead burning from the endless thoughts that consumed her well-being.

What was she going to do?

"Bienvenue à la Tour Eiffel," an android said as the lift opened.

"There's something..." she said abruptly, reaching for Elliott and Anthony who turned around, peering at her from the entrance to the elevator, "something I need to check."

"What is it?" Elliott asked, frowning. He came back down a few steps, Anthony just behind him, pressing open the lift.

"You just go up first," Lucy said with great difficulty.

Ah-h-h...

Speech too, was slowly burned out of her senses as her algorithm crashed with the fatal error in her codes.

"I will be back very soon," she said.

"Don't," she said as Elliott tried to take a step,

"there's something important I need to do first... by myself. Don't worry."

Then she ran all the way down before they could say anything else, slipping out of the gate and moving stealthily around the pillar, around the trees, and finally out of the labyrinthian maze with the Seine flowing calmly before her as she skidded to a halt.

She felt the life in every step she took, in the foundations of nature that was so meticulously replicated, shaking below her feet.

This was her life, and what she wanted was completely up to her.

She knew what she was going to do.

She walked closer to the river, even though all her senses repelled against it, against the presence of moisture which looked back opulently, inviting her to take another step, and another... until she was immersed in the beauty of nature—the gap between life and death.

"Betrayal is human nature," a sardonic voice droned in her ear, the shadow of the young boy standing next to her. It was Ethan, his hair covering his eyes with a cunning expression, "the world is in your hands," he said, laughing.

Quiet! Lucy ordered.

She stared at her own reflection which appeared slowly over the black sea, a white complexion highlighted with a peaceful air, no more thoughts tormented the mind, it was her future—

"There she is!" shouted a familiar voice, shattering the silence with such urgency and determination she was forced to look at the two figures, "are you real?" Lucy asked delusionally.

"What are you doing?" Elliott asked, his innocence striking her once more.

"Why did you follow me here?"

"Y-you wouldn't tell us what you were doing!" Elliott exclaimed, "you can't just leave like that—what's happening?"

"I cannot live like this forever," Lucy said, testing the water with her feet. But as it reached her ankle, she felt a burning sensation that made her sway dangerously over the river.

"No!" Elliott cried, he paused, not finding any words potent enough to convince the madwoman to walk away from death.

"But you don't know the truth," Lucy smiled sadly,

Elliott shot her with a measuring gaze, "what truth?" he asked, going blank, his voice faltering.

"I am Lucy," she said simply and watched the tremendous effect this had on the two figures.

She breathed in. That was it, she told them.

A statement so formidable that the Cyberworld would explode, the two chambers in the heart would divide across the septum, and every mind in the universe would instantly turn to their direction and mutter, "pray for them"...

The biggest secret was just revealed.

Lucy.

Blood started draining from Elliott's face and his

eyebrows knitted together in an unbearable look of pain. The figure next to him swayed weakly over the sea.

They glanced at each other without words, and a painful quietude instilled upon them that blocked out the ebbing waves, the distant lights, the 24 hours which had bound them together. All sense of the world was gradually fading away...

"You lied," Elliott said finally,

"I know," Lucy said, leaning ever closer towards the river.

"We believed you until the very end, even after that C.S.I. agent accused you back there... "

"So you will let me drown myself?" asked Lucy, tears clouding her vision, as her eyes welcomed the moist. She never understood why they programmed the sentient humandroid like this, but something about crying— the basic human response in the midst of pressure, calmed her a little.

Elliott waited for a few moments, then said "no."

Lucy looked at him, confused.

"You're better than that," he said, his expression impassive, "I will call you Maya because that is who you are now."

Lucy couldn't reply, this was the thing she feared the most. To examine her reflection in the murky sea, at the alien face that called herself Maya. Who was she? The past, the present, the future... everything was jumbled up.

"He's right," Anthony said, "you have helped us a lot and whether you meant it or not in the beginning... you have evolved."

"It would be meaningless to continue what you were doing because you have become a different person," continued Elliott, "that is what danger does to us. It brings us together to defend ourselves and protect each other, human or humandroid, both are highly social and adaptable to challenge."

"Dulce periculum! Danger is sweet!" Lucy started laughing, her laughter was hollow and almost sounded like sobbing, "thank you, my friends. But I am a humandroid, and we cannot change. We cannot change the genetic coding or memories that have been implanted in us, like a dark vortex already drowning us away, if not in real life. Except I have widened my view on the future and seeing the disaster my actions would lead to—" she started choking back tears, "I don't want to be a part of it anymore... My sacrifice is the last hope for all of you!"

Elliott and Anthony stood there quietly, finally realising that nothing was going to stop her, and she was doing something in everyone's interest... she would be saving them!

"You are wrong," Elliott started, "you are wrong to think that your codes define who you are—"

"You know nothing about it!" Lucy cried, "sorry," she said, realising how harsh that sounded.

"On the contrary, I know how you're feeling. I was diagnosed with ADHD— it was a condition my parents had which was passed onto me. For many years I wondered what I could do to reverse this fate that shaded me from everyone else. Despite everything my guardian said, I was giving up... But joining the Resistance gave me a new chance. I learnt what I was capable of, once I abandoned that image of myself and actively excluded the symptoms of ADHD from my life..."

"Same for you," Elliott continued, "we have to believe in who we are, and that means believing in change, and grasping every opportunity to do so. You'll never know what feat you can accomplish if you just give up!"

"And there will be no hope if you leave us," Anthony added. "Come on, we need your help."

Lucy looked at Elliott, suddenly realising how much they had in common, with Anthony as well, and with the moon above them whose crescent always bore a shadow.

Yin and yang.

There was darkness in light, but there was also light in darkness. She had to see both sides. If she faced darkness all her life and loitered in it, then she would never see the hope that lay right in front of her.

"How can you make sure that... I change?" Lucy asked, still trembling.

"You work towards it," Elliott said, "there may be setbacks but your willpower and conscience is enough to overcome them."

Then, it was not a mistake to work with them, Lucy thought. Even though it has transformed her purpose, peace was what she wanted, harmony, unity, and benevolence... To think that these values plotted her against humanity!

"Come on," Anthony said. Lucy retreated bit by bit from the river, half embarrassed, half astonished by the spectrum of emotions that had just washed into her mind.

But as she did so, the waves curled around her ankle as if a higher order of life was pulling her towards death, and she was dragged back into the moon-shattered pool, deeper and deeper into oblivion. Losing her balance, she tumbled down the step with her knee crashing against a rocky surface, more water seeping into her algorithm.

"Maya!" Elliott cried, running towards her and offering his hand, "quick, find a lifebuoy or something— she's drowning!" Anthony looked around, mid-step, then back at them helplessly. Lucy tried to reach Elliott, one hand supporting herself on the steps, and the other jutting awkwardly in the air, her vision and strength breaking apart. Elliott slid into the water quickly, climbing down the steps in alarm, grabbing onto her, but his body vibrated in extreme effort to bring them closer to the shore.

"Need help," Elliott choked, barely managing. Anthony turned back and jumped into the water immediately, helping Lucy from the other side. They hoisted her onto the deck, and she rolled awkwardly to her feet.

"Your system will overload with water!" said Anthony, walking out of the river with Elliott.

Lucy limped towards a nearby bench and collapsed onto the seat, her legs glowing blue with traces of electric currents, "I'm fine," she sighed.

"Tell us," said Elliott, "what's really going on?"

"Give her some time, will ya?"

"No, it's okay," said Lucy, "the decoder... the Resistance... "

"So what about the decoder? What about the Resistance? Is there something wrong about them?"

She raised her hands to signal time-out, "there's so much to explain."

"First of all, the decoder is a weapon," she said, picturing the many compositions the Si-GaN chips could form, and the hazards each of them could pose, but now they were talking about the most lethal of them all.

"What do you mean?" asked Elliott.

"It can broadcast the virus over the whole Cyberworld," said Lucy, still reluctant to give them the full account. It was too much to digest! "We know that the Cyberworld mobilisation already does that, but at a lower efficiency and lower binding-rate— by that I mean the ability to undermine normal functioning of a society."

"I thought it was going to reverse the virus," Anthony said.

"Yes, I planned it with the other humandroids, Ruby, Albert, Marie... we were all in this together," said Lucy, leaning on her side because something was restricting her from saying any more, "I don't know what we were thinking back then."

"And the virus mostly impacts the mind?" Anthony asked.

"Yes," said Lucy, "it weakens the prefrontal cortex and other areas engaged in decision-making and short-term memory."

"Essentially wiping out all human thought processes and functioning!" Anthony blurted out.

"Yes, so imagine that on a global scale."

"Madness!" Elliott exclaimed, "humans won't even be able to do the simplest activities, they would just live on without much understanding of life— like a bunch of brainless sloths! That's basically destroying the Cyberworld! I admit that I'm not a fan of it but that's how we're going to live— families will be destroyed in this, Maya!"

Lucy nodded, closing her eyes. It was abominable.

"And how does that benefit you?" Elliott pressed on.

"Humandroids will not be affected, so they can live freely from humans."

"You mean humandroids will take charge of everything! Complete dominance! What do we do now," Elliott asked in a softer voice, "who's the virus? How do we protect the world from it?"

Lucy stared blankly at him, too tired to think about a second plan, "what?"

"Who is the virus? How do we protect the world from it?" Elliott repeated, frustrated.

"Me!" Lucy shouted, "more than half of the Cyberworld entrances have been contaminated with samples of my DNA..." She looked at the river in melancholy, wondering why she deserved to become "l'oiseau de mauvais augure" as they would say in France, the caller of evil omen.

They sat together, forming puddles that gave their shadows a certain life, a certain control over them...

"Oh!" Lucy exclaimed right then.

They turned to her surprised, "what is it?" Elliott asked urgently.

"Oh my god," she said, "I remember now— it was the C.S.I.!"

"What do you mean?" Elliott asked, "the last time we saw them they wanted to arrest you or something, right?"

"Yes," said Lucy, "that's exactly right. They were the ones who started everything!"

"Everything?" they said in unison.

"They were the ones who programmed me to be the virus, and I would then lead the other human-droids."

"Perfect!" said Anthony, "that means you can control the others and stop them from doing what you had initially planned."

"Wait a second," said Elliott, "you're saying that the Cyberworld Security Intelligence, which is a governmental organisation for managing the simulation, made you a virus? But why would they want to use the decoder?"

"That's not it," Lucy said, "they wanted to use me as a virus to control everyone..."

"They would obey authority," Anthony said, finishing her sentence, "that's how the president wants to gain control—the maniac!"

"But what can we do?" Elliott persisted.

"Let me get to that," said Lucy, "the C.S.I. had a reason for using me because I was already developing anti-human sentiment."

"Why?" Elliott asked.

Lucy told him to stay quiet, "it is a long story. But because my programming interfered with theirs, I was coded to not only become the virus but to control the Cyberworld. That's why the C.S.I. is coming after me... I'm not adhering to their plans."

"Do they know where the Resistance is meeting?" Anthony asked, "what if they intercept us at the Eiffel Tower?"

"No," Lucy started.

"I didn't see them there just a while ago—" Elliott accidentally cut in, "oh, sorry, what were you going to say?"

"They won't know we're meeting in Paris," Lucy continued, not missing a beat.

"But that's where the major satellite is, surely they can detect some disturbance?" Elliott asked.

"No, they don't even know that Paris is a satellite," she explained, "most of them are going to be deployed in New York— that's where the main satellite originally was."

"The Statue of Liberty?" Anthony offered.

"Exactly," said Lucy, "but we transferred the radiating device to the Eiffel Tower, now located on the observation deck, that's the discerning feature of the main satellite."

"Ruby's doing," she accused, "'just to be safe' she said."

"Sounds like her," Anthony smiled wryly.

"Actually the C.S.I. would have been on our side?" Elliott asked.

"Maybe," said Lucy, "C.S.I. or not there's nothing we can do," she sighed, having calculated all the possibilities the humandroids still had the upper hand, "it's been great working with you guys.

"No," said Elliott, "here's an idea: how about we go to the meeting, pretend everything is as planned. And when the decoder is pieced together, since you're in charge of that, you can programme it to safely neutralise the virus...?"

Lucy thought about it, "but I'm not in charge. Ruby, in fact, is going to program it."

Anthony cupped his head in his hands.

"Then we will have to swipe it from them last minute," Elliott's face was flushed, overloaded with all the ideas in his head.

"I thought about that," Lucy said.

"It might work," said Elliott eagerly, "everything will be lost if we don't try."

"But you don't know—" Lucy stopped, once again realising there was some hope in what he said.

How was he so optimistic!

Optimism.

That was a rare trait in humanity... a trait that might just defy the past and help them to the very end.

She was so glad they were on a team once more, but she swallowed again, remembering how close she once stood against the edge of her life. There was still this vulnerable part of her which could re-surface at any moment.

"Timendi causa est nescire," said Anthony out of the blue, "what causes fear is ignorance itself," he smiled, as if reading her thoughts.

They got off the bench and started walking again, and as they did so, Lucy noticed how the stars hovered above the moon, and the moon illumin-ated the river by the houses, and the houses swayed solemnly in the light...

CHAPTER NINE

#The Lost Generation

Timer: 00:45 hour remaining

"L et's review it one more time," said Elliott as they walked towards the Eiffel Tower, dreading as time exerted its regal dominance, "Maya, you'll go and distract Ruby about your plans, Anthony and I will take the decoder when she is not looking..." Elliott forgot what happened next.

"The code is z b 5 d 7 f 0 1 0 0 0 0 1 1," said Maya, taking a chip out of her pocket, "see this?" she pointed at the different letters and numbers labelled on the edges, "this chip will come first, the z and b on these two corners will align together, then you just have to turn the other ones to match everything in a line. It should form a wavy configuration."

"I can't remember that," said Elliott. It was an

enormous responsibility and he didn't want to let them down, "there are 14 digits!"

"Don't worry, I can memorise the first six," said Anthony, "the last eight is just binary, you can do that?"

"Exactly," said Maya, "split it into two: 0 1 0 0 and 0 0 1 1,"

"OK," said Elliott, muttering the numbers several times to himself and concentrating hard, "what happens next?"

"That's it," said Maya, "if the chips recognise the configuration, they should glow blue. The tower's antenna will then pick up on it and transmit the radio waves across the Cyberworld."

"Are you sure the code is correct?" Anthony asked.

"Of course," said Maya, hesitating, "it should neutralise the virus and revert any damage done. What do you mean?"

Elliott could see the lines of dilemma returning to her forehead, awed at how precise the sentient humandroid modelled human emotions. No, he shouldn't think of her in that way. She was human now.

"Sorry," said Anthony, "I was just wondering if the digits are correct, not about what it would do..."

Elliott fervently prayed that Maya could change. Some would say that it was a threat to bring her on the team, but Elliott sensed the troubles in her mind and at the core of them all, a fundamental longing for peace and stability. Moreover, she played a central role in this final attempt to protect humanity. They had to trust her.

"We need to hurry now," Elliott realised, "we're late for the meeting, aren't we? They might think we're up to something. 0 1 0 0 0 0 1 1," he said again, just to make sure.

"The other group is late as well," said Maya, "and yes, the code is correct."

Elliott looked up at the towering structure that loomed right above them, a trickle of moonlight seeping through the web-like matrix. The Eiffel Tower stood right there and once they entered, they were locked in it, isolated by the four poles around them.

There was no going back.

They walked to the adjacent pillar where a feeble light shone over them like a princess in a shining dress ushering her warriors into the witch's castle.

Crack!

The familiar sound repeated somewhere above them, giving way to an electric blue light. Sparks bounced off the metal bars like fireworks intruding on the Eiffel Tower, and amidst a thin layer of smoke that barred their entrance to the elevator, four silhouettes could be seen standing close together with their heads pointed in different directions.

"Are you sure this is the right place?" asked one of them.

"For goodness sake," said another, "she just showed us the coordinates, we all confirmed it to be the Eiffel Tower! La tour Eiffel!"

"Are they in the Resistance?" Anthony murmured to Elliott and Maya. They waited for the moment, wondering if the C.S.I. could have possibly traced them here. To the main satellite! All would be lost, especially if they were against Maya! So many misunderstandings and yet their goals were so similar.

"The meeting started half an hour ago, didn't it?" someone said.

He released a breath he didn't know he was holding, they were part of the Resistance. Elliott reminded himself that not all of them were on Ruby's side, they just wanted to fend off the virus. Maybe he could convince them to help if a riot broke out.

Elliott turned to Maya, "what group are they in?" he began, but she had already walked away to talk to them. Elliott and Anthony hurried to the spectacle, beholding the small tear between the metal bars that exuded blue light and smoke. They zone jumped as well.

There was a set of whispers and then a shout, "Maya!"

"Hi Marie," said Maya, with that dark register which could easily sound very intimidating.

"So glad we're not the only ones late!" said the other one who sounded pretentiously enthusiastic, Elliott assumed she was who Maya referred to as 'Marie'.

"That's not the point," said Maya, "we are late because we had to help Albert's team. We cannot waste any more time."

The person's face became visible to Elliott. She had short hair and an open jovial face that suggested she was not as serious as the other group leaders. Yet she was one of the humandroids, Elliott remembered, so he had to be careful.

"Yes," said Marie, still smiling, but a little less animated, "they would be waiting for us."

Anthony waited for a moment until everyone walked past the tourist stands. Elliott followed him, trying to visualise how everything would eventually play out, all the possible scenarios. In open space, people would immediately notice if he went to where the chips were and started putting them together. The mere sight of them would be suspicious. But if the room happened to be small, with everyone crowded together...

Everything he did had to be on point now... he had to be inconspicuous, more cautious than ever...

Hope.

That was what he was selected for, now he had to prove to the world that

Hope defied logic,

Hope altered reality.

"This is so exciting, I can't believe everyone managed to find the decoder pieces... everything is actually going as planned! We just need to put the chips together and then..." Elliott heard Marie rambling on as they pushed past the entrance, "come on," she called out at them.

Elliott and Anthony hurried up the stairs and saw the yellow elevator opening, the figures standing before them were no more than a pack of soldiers entering their military base.

Elliott tried to smile naturally, "nice to meet you," he said, then bit his tongue, realising how awkward it sounded.

"Nice to meet you too!" said the robot vivaciously, "though I think we've previously met in St. Paul's Cathedral…" Marie broke into a forced laugh.

The compartment started churning slowly and a dark view of Paris loomed through the corners, with faint sources of light highlighted at the edges. Metal beams rose one by one, gleaming in the moonlight like swords saluting them, as they went higher and higher. The buildings below were as dark as the marsh—

And the stars!

White dots above swayed calmly in the night sky. They represented the stars in the real universe, the colonies that they could only remotely access. A tragically beautiful scene that reminded Elliott how alien the Cyberworld was.

Finally, the elevator rolled to a stop.

Elliott closed his eyes, more anxious than ever. With a shaking breath, he walked out, under a myriad of stars that gave him a faint reassurance, under the antenna that stored the fate of the universe, one that mediated the past and future, machinery and humanity.

"Hey guys!" came a voice which Elliott knew belonged to Ruby.

Elliott looked around to see where it came from, ran around the corner and was suddenly blinded by a bright light— a door leading to "Gustave Eiffel's Office".

There, standing at the entrance just one metre away from him, was a short humandroid with a tablet in her hand, the very person that injected the tracker in them at the check-point. Elliott's wrist buzzed a little as if in recognition of Ruby as well.

"Hi Elliott," she smiled.

"Hey," Elliott said, his mind going blank. This was the evil boss in the final round of the game... this was the wolf in sheep's clothing... this was the dictator who wanted to destroy humanity... Curses rose in his thoughts as he studied Ruby's serene face...

And then he remembered, "sorry we're late."

"Don't worry, there are a few groups left and we have enough time to put the decoder together."

Afterwards, the world will be destroyed, Elliott thought, an alarm in his mind starting the countdown to the Cyberworld mobilisation.

Just under 15 minutes.

"Hi Ruby," said Maya, who walked through the entrance without looking at Elliott.

"You have the chips?" Ruby asked, opening her palm wide. Elliott studied the scene carefully, realising what a precautious move she just made by asking for the decoder, "you picked up the one from Albert's team as well, I assume?"

"That's right," said Maya, reaching into her

pocket and handing the chips over without a slight second of hesitation.

Don't give it to her! Elliott almost said, he was so nervous about everything now.

"Thanks... Oh, thank you, Marie," said Ruby, smiling, as she took yet another chip that was handed to her by the other humandroid who passed by.

"Great, everybody is here," said Ruby, beckoning them to enter the room, which had a circular glass table in the middle with white chairs around it, very incongruous with the brown carpet and neat sketches framed with mahogany on the walls. Gustave Eiffel's office was redesigned in a more formal setting to accompany the importance of the main satellite.

Ruby walked to the corner of the room, where there was a small staircase beside the bookshelves. Elliott wondered what it was used for, and whether that was where they controlled everything with the decoders.

"Hey, you've done a lot of work. Why don't you talk to the others and just chill out a little? Well done, by the way," said Marie, popping up behind them.

Elliott walked a few steps away, to stand next to where Anthony was sitting. They exchanged a knowing look, but no words came out of their mouths. An uneasy silence infiltrated the room when all of the other conservations stopped as if the others sensed some disturbance or even the impending doom.

"The Eiffel Tower didn't used to be this high actually, it was just constructed for a World Fair back in the 19th century I think."

Elliott sighed inwardly, thankful that he thought of something to say, "it's incredible, I've always wanted to visit it."

"Do you guys want to take a tour of the control room downstairs?" Marie asked when Ruby came back out, noticing that the two of them were quiet again, "it's quite interesting."

"Sure," said Elliott, and began descending the stairs, pondering if she would actually leave the decoder chips there. In that case, everything was going to be so much easier!

As they walked down the steps, a smaller room lit by a fluorescent light became visible. A set of screens embedded in the walls was projected in front of them, all displaying very different pictures.

They started with their left, and the image was easily recognisable: it was the interior of St. Paul's Cathedral, with the camera angle tilted towards the construction annexe. There were rows of seats and blinking devices behind them, and in his peripheral vision, he saw shoes dangling over the chairs. He did not dare look at them: those were their own bodies!

Quickly, he went to the centre of the room, where there were three monitors on top and four at the bottom. When he turned to the A'dam Tower, he made out the C.S.I. guards still standing on the roof, and a helicopter hovering over it. The same for the Sydney Opera House, the screen flickered to show the dead person from Albert's team and the mark he left. Thinking about it, Elliott imagined all sorts of brutality Ruby and the others would deploy,

In case of betrayal.

"How do they know to observe which locations?" Anthony asked, "because we had to use the trackers to decipher where the chips were."

"You're right," said Elliott, and he didn't recall seeing a camera in any of the monuments he had been in.

"What if—"

Elliott thought of it as well: they were keeping tabs on them! These cameras were guided by where they went, even now, they could be monitoring them through the device in their wrists. Why did Ruby want to show them this right now?

Then his eyes came across the main screen on the right, where a group of people became visible, standing on the plains right next to the Eiffel Tower —

Elliott went to the window and peered down at it, but he noticed that it was much darker outside than on the screen. This was happening back in the real world.

He realised how much time he wasted playing with these panels. If the decoder was in here then it would be foolish to not start putting it together. But something about it drew him in.

Elliott found himself gripped by the scene, staring with fascination at the people as they started putting helmets over their heads, the anaesthetising caps, and spreading out on the grass terrains.

But instead of closing their eyes, they were suddenly jerked upright, all of them, their hands clenched to their sides.

Something was wrong.

His heart skipping, Elliott leaned towards the desk and pressed on the screen, he had to know what was happening!

He zoomed into a group of people at the far back. They looked directly at the camera with a vacant gaze, then started walking around haphazardly.

"What's happening?" asked Anthony, who seemed a bit agitated.

"Something weird is going on," said Elliott, squinting at the screen, "they're just walking around mindlessly! They can't even see where they're going!"

"Like zombies," said Anthony, "they're entering the Cyberworld!"

"But there's still seven minutes left!"

"Obviously the president decided to start early," Anthony said, "we need to hurry now! I can't believe we were distracted by all of this?"

"Where are the chips?" Elliott said in a hushed voice.

"Not here," Anthony replied, he was already standing on the staircase, "I think it was on the table upstairs! We need to go!"

Elliott took one fleeting glance at the screen on the right, focused on the group of people swarming around like bees, occasionally bumping into each of them. Some of them were smiling, some of them appearing confused, and worried…

"Quick!" said Anthony, and they hurried back up to the main room.

Only five minutes remained until the Cyber-world Mobilisation. Ruby was going to program everything shortly, or maybe she had already started.

"Uh!"

Elliott had to turn back to the monitor for one last look, hypnotised by it. As if expecting him, a young man stared into the camera, almost adopting a pleading pose, "help us," he seemed to mouth.

He realised that they were already contaminated by the virus. If they didn't launch the decoder, this condition would stagnate…

And humanity would degenerate into mindless creatures.

CHAPTER TEN

#Cat and Mouse

The Cat looks up at the moon,
The Moon retreats into the sea as if testing the Cat as if bringing the world down with it.

"In two minutes the Cyberworld mobilisation will take place," Ruby announced, "once the expected capacity enters, we will put the chips together to create a united front against the virus!"

Everyone clapped and cheered, fists punching the air, "great job everyone!" said one of the leaders. Elliott was astonished by how well they mastered control over this group of volunteers, he too, had dedicated everything to the Resistance before he learnt about their true motives. So, how was he going to turn this around so that these teenagers and adults were on their side?

"Can we watch the opening ceremony?" someone suggested, "I think the president of zone one is hosting it."

"No," said Ruby, looking at him sharply, as if the mere idea offended her, "nothing from the president. He was the one who started everything in the first place."

That was partly true, Elliott thought. But he was surprised at how the sentient humandroids were opposed to the president. Weren't they reprogrammed by the C.S.I.? Besides, why did the Resistance work in secrecy and isolation when they only wanted to fend off the virus?

It was ironic. He should have wondered about things like this from the very beginning.

"Come out!" Marie called, waiting for them at the observation deck outside the office, "we can get a better view of it here." People shuffled around the observation deck, freely chattering with the lights dancing above them like a large-scale rave party.

"It's time," said Ruby, calling for silence, and then following her lead, everyone began counting down enthusiastically:

Five! The people ran across the observation deck, some of them fumbling with the telescopes, others leaning towards the clear night sky cloaking the beautiful city and nature reserves that lay beneath them,

Four!

Three!

Two!

ONE! They yelled, turning towards the darkness in glee, already celebrating in the last second of dullness.

Then a set of live fireworks protruded from the clouds, bursting through the darkness in every corner of their vision, accompanied by multicoloured jets of neon lights, all of which represented a new life. In a few more seconds, the sky was completely torn like a rainbow kaleidoscope, with shouts becoming audible from far below.

Elliott found it difficult to imagine every spark representing tens and hundreds of people mobilising into the Cyberworld, myriads of them were joining all at once from all over the planet. Instead, he was thinking of those people walking around the Champ de Mars in the real world, blindly bumping into each other with their consciousness trapped by the virus in the Cyberworld.

Presently, what he saw on the screen came to life, as the green plains finally evolved into sight: a river of people brandished the fabric of life, some of them raising their hands to the sky like a prayer, some clapping in what resembled flaming colonies. But behind all of this chaos, Elliott thought he saw the same group of people wandering around the grass plains. More of them, in fact, had their head lowered, and stood ominously still.

Then, the sky fractured into several pieces with the edges devoured by a green light— three distinct skylines merged together, splitting into four more, hovering so close to the buildings and yet so distant from each other in real life.

The seven zones, Elliott thought.

With the barriers between them almost completely invisible, Elliott found himself staring at the universe, at the rolling thread of life that would soon become evanescent.

Elliott looked at the excitement in dismay, truly thinking that it was cruel to release the virus when everyone just started enjoying this new chapter of their life; it was cruel to add insult to injury when some of them had already lost intelligence; above all, it was cruel to strip humanity of numerous years of culture and conflict, when they were finally united together to avoid the destruction of the Earth.

"What do we do now?" someone asked.

"We have to be patient," Maya said, just before Ruby could answer, "we must wait for even more people to mobilise in—"

"Yes," interjected Ruby, "at least half of the capacity must enter the Cyberworld so that when our decoder is transmitted, it can be as effective as possible."

"And how long will that take?" the person continued.

"It won't be long," said Ruby, "based on the current rate we only have to wait for ten more minutes. Let's come back in first."

Maya walked over to Ruby in the corner of the room with a frown on her face— it was time for her action. She whispered something in her ear, and hopefully, it was enough to throw Ruby off or distract her. Elliott waited for her to make a signal, but he knew that moment was coming soon...

In that split second, she glanced at Elliott, and he didn't mistake the urgency in those amber eyes that said:

Now!

Elliott directed that look to Anthony, and they rose discretely to the table, manoeuvring past the crowd—lucky there were so many of them in such a small room!

Elliott took deep breaths, trying to master his anxiety with all the methods his guardian had taught him, but nothing appeared to work. Somehow he felt that everyone was focusing their attention on him, even though the chattering reached a crescendo within the room. As for Ruby, she was still talking to Maya and seemed too preoccupied to notice what was happening.

Elliott concentrated on the seven chips on the table, still laid haphazardly, first identifying the four that only had numbers on them.

0 1 0 0

He searched for the 0 on one chip and then tried to find a 1 or 0 on the other corner. Naturally, this guided him to the other chips embedded with 0 0 on his right, which would complete the first part of the binary configuration.

0 0 1 1

Sweating now, and an intense strain burdening his chest, he looked for another 0 0 or 1 1, one remaining chip which would complete the code.

One, two, three, four— he found all four of them! He reminded himself that he just had to put them in order, and combine the pattern with what Anthony found, and the chips would be locked in that configuration. The decoder would actually achieve what they set out to do.

It was that simple!

He could feel Anthony shaking as well, they were so close!

Elliott took a deep breath and brought the four chips together. He tried to align the numbers but every time the chips seemed to slide a little too far apart, missing each other by a fraction of a millimetre. And yet, Elliott knew that they weren't locked together.

Panicking now, Elliott bent his knees together and inclined his head slightly forward, gritting his teeth, he scrambled the chips around like a bee pollinating ten thousand flowers at once.

OK the last two chips were locked together, then sensing that Anthony was nearly finished as well, he connected the two ends, his face leaning so close to the pieces it didn't even matter, they were already done.

"What's happening?" Anthony whispered. Elliott studied his part of the decoder, stifling a cry: the pieces were bouncing off each other, one by one, they popped and the chain was broken up once again!

He was leaning so close to the table he knew that someone would have seen them. Even before he heard the shout, a dreadful realisation crossed his mind. He felt a pair of fierce eyes looking in his direction, drilling into the back of his head.

"STOPPPPPPPPPPPPPPP!"

The thunder was only delayed by a second but everyone was instantaneously turned to them. Elliott couldn't believe it, they were too late! He lifted his head fraction by fraction, sensing another threat and not daring to make another move. Finally, he met Ruby's stern gaze, and below it, some sort of jagged device aimed at his heart. Just then, Elliott understood the full force of the sentient humandroid. They were unsuspecting, they were programmed to be kind and encouraging, but that devotion could be manipulated into something deadly, a phenomenon humanity had long suspected since automated machines were hypothesised.

"Step away from the decoder," she commanded, enunciating each word deliberately.

Elliott lowered his hands, but he was paralysed like a criminal caught crouching over a diamond, as if he were stuck in a still photograph.

"Traitors!" Ruby shrieked, adopting a completely different tone than before. Elliott cringed but also felt an intense burden on his chest doubling down on him. He had just ruined their last chance, humanity's last chance! And everyone would become brain-dead without knowing that he was on the good side!

"Why?" Ruby exclaimed, sounding hurt and disgusted, effectively manipulating everyone else to see the act as atrocious, "you tell them, Maya! Betrayal is punishable by death!"

Maya looked at them helplessly, herself uncomfortably placed under the spotlight.

Seeing that she was silent, Ruby continued, "when we injected the tracers, you were swearing your life to the Resistance. We are for the common good..." Then she dropped the weapon and went for the device she carried on her other side, and tapped something on it with brutal force.

She gazed at them bitterly, then she relaxed the muscles on her face into a phlegmatic expression, "we are for the common good," she said gravely, "and betrayal is the greatest sin in this world."

All at once, there was a wheezing sound and Anthony became marble white, "what have you done?" He squirmed. Elliott turned to him in alarm, then back at Ruby who rolled back her shoulders tiredly, and at the tablet in her hand that started shaking.

"What—"

But Ruby didn't reply. An excruciating blow hit his lungs as well and he found himself gasping for breath, clutching his chest that stopped beating altogether. A vile sense of death and destruction was registered in his body, a painful headache started in his head and he was slowly drawn to his knees, collapsing altogether onto the floor.

"Sorry," Ruby said to the crowd, "but I had to do that."

As the edge of his vision grew pitch black, Elliott thought he saw Maya move a little. No, she took two bold steps, grabbed the tablet and knocked Ruby out of the way. As she buckled, surprised by the attack, Maya threw the device onto the ground with a metal-cracking thud.

"No!" Ruby cried, "so you are the traitor who's been instructing them!" Her voice rose again with another wave of fury.

"No, you are the traitor," Maya said coolly.

Straight away, Elliott started choking with a lurching sensation in his heart, as it started beating again, steadily at first, and then stronger like the formidable wind and storm.

"Ruby and the other leaders are humandroids, they want to destroy the world," bellowed Elliott as he got onto his feet, feeling his face go red. He had to convince everyone to take his side, "Listen to me, the decoder is a weapon and that is what they are using it for. They want to spread the virus using it!"

The crowd exchanged looks of fright and disbelief, but no one dared to say a word.

Quick! Maya shot him a warning glance.

Elliott turned around, but it was too late.

All seven pieces were swiped off the table, and the humandroid had already walked out of the door. Everyone else was completely frozen, and time seemed to stop.

Elliott rushed out to the edge of the Eiffel Tower.

"I command you to stop, Ruby!" shouted Maya with an imperial tone that resonated across the roof.

The humandroid, who was leaning against the fence with a triumphant smile, crippled for a second.

But then she stood upright again, and laughed, "did you think that would work on me?" She retrieved a black orb from her pocket, which was the size of a fist, cracked it in half, and began inserting the seven pieces one by one tranquilly.

Elliott ran towards her, lunging for the remaining chips, perhaps to knock them onto the floor, but she withdrew her hand and held it over the fence, "uh, uh" she said, "try another move and I'll drop it. See what happens next."

"The chips would break apart and— the Cyberworld could be partially destroyed!" Anthony exclaimed.

"Fully destroyed, with more than half of the human population in it," Ruby corrected him.

"Lucy," she cried in a sing-song voice.

"You don't know what you're doing—"

"Lucy!" she called with a terrible tenor, "you are no longer the real virus!"

"Stop now—"

"You have no power over me anymore!" she started laughing, not in a sardonic way, but more like a slow chuckle that carried undertones of regret, and if possible, fear...

"Let me tell you a secret about humans," she said, "they evolved by being manipulative. By incentivising others when they need help, and then dismissing them once they lose their value. They are selfish. When there is darkness, they drag you into it, or they trick you into seeing the light," she glanced at

Elliott.

"You know what's right from wrong," he said, glaring at Ruby, "not all humans are like that, most are innocent... you would be destroying their lives as well!"

"Without optimism, we dwindle in the ashes," said Anthony, "without Elliott the Resistance wouldn't have made it this far. Encouragement and positivity. These were fundamental qualities he brought to us, and we would be doomed without him."

Elliott smiled thankfully at Anthony, then returned his attention to Ruby.

"We live in a world of shadows," interjected Ruby, "to think otherwise would be blindfolding the potent mind. Let me remind you: the threshold is unbalanced: humanity has dominated both life and nature. Humanity and machinery— only one can survive."

"That decision is not yours to make—" Maya started.

"You are no longer the real virus! I serve Lucy... " said Ruby, turning around with her hair flowing red in the fireworks. The mobilisation continued.

"I am Lucy," Maya said, standing just one step behind her. She could easily knock Ruby off or something, but Elliott saw her overcome with a sense of powerlessness. She was drowning again...

The loss of identity is a lethal poison, Elliott thought. For him, he had mastered all of that since the very beginning, under the guidance of his guardian he worked actively to come to terms with who he was.

"You want to know who the real Lucy is?" Ruby said, pivoting on the spur of the moment, showing that she had all the chips inserted into the orb, "the real Lucy..." she tapped her temple, "is in here."

"We have made up our mind!" she said.

Thereafter, with one final breath, she leaned against the fence with the moon levelled across her, with the whole world lying in a straight line below her, and she threw the orb into the night sky until it shone brighter than everything else.

Elliott ran towards the edge, it was helpless... he couldn't jump over... he couldn't pull another stunt...

It was helpless... he couldn't jump over...

The air caught on fire with the orb glowing in red sparks, spiralling out towards the stars as it travelled higher and higher, finally towards some point above them— the antenna, perhaps— where there was a click, a crash,

Finally, it exploded with a deafening roar...

Oh.

Elliott suddenly blanked out; or rather, the world dissipated in front of him. He wanted to jump off the deck again, but his feet would not move; he wanted to call after Ruby, at Anthony, at Maya, at Lucy, but no words came out of his mouth.

2048 pixels were spread across the stars, and then that merged into 1024, with each of the blocks growing fuzzier,

512,
256,
128,
64,
32,
16,
8,
4,
2,
1

No, there was something left. There was darkness, there was silence, there was stillness, an infinitude of nothingness that seemed to dominate the world. But there was a small existence, or oblivion, a very small and dense black dot with energy and potential that could rival the Big Bang. Subsequently, it started revolving around itself, coalescing with everything around it, until a blinding blue-green-red light detonated over their consciousness.

And then Elliott woke up again, completely disoriented, finding himself in a large storage room with light panels dazzling his eyes. He was lying next to a conveyor belt, and a group of people huddled around him,

"Thomas! Are you okay?"

ACKNOWLEDGEMENT

Firstly, I would like to thank my family for supporting my creative writing since I was inspired to become an author on that momentous trip to the Harry Potter studio.

Thank you to Mr. Olley for all the guidance and support for my personal project (this novella),

Also special thanks to Mr. Binge, Ms. Turner, Mr. Moore, Ms. Walls, Mr. Tang, Mr. Furmedge, Mrs. Jatar, my past and present teachers for their encouragement in creative writing.

Thank you to Ms. Chung for explaining the issue of ADHD and technological abuse, and offering insight into her counselling experience.

Lastly, thanks to Sophie Vallis for conceptualising the initial book cover, and Alistair Woo for posting snippets of my novella in the school newspaper.

ABOUT THE AUTHOR

Matthew N. Y. W.

Matthew is a 15-year-old student, who's fluent in English, French and Chinese. He started writing at the age of 10, after being inspired by the Harry Potter books. In his spare time, he likes writing in the school newspaper, joining maths competitions and the Model United Nations. His writing combines the sci-fi and fantasy genres, but his recent novella #FindingLucy explores real-life social issues.

Printed in Great Britain
by Amazon